The Great Big Demon Hunting Agency

by

Peter Oxley

Burning Chair Limited, Trading As Burning Chair Publishing
61 Bridge Street, Kington HR5 3DJ

www.burningchairpublishing.com

By Peter Oxley
Edited by Simon Finnie
Cover by Jake Clark

First published by Burning Chair Publishing, 2023

ISBN: 978-1-912946-33-4

THE GREAT BIG DEMON HUNTING AGENCY

Also by Peter Oxley

Chapter One

London, 1868

Tap-tap, tap-tap.

Mist plucked at the woman's heels as she made her way down the darkened street, the houses to either side leaning in on her like bent-backed old crones. She pulled her coat tighter around her body as she picked up her pace, as much to defend herself against the cold as from the unseen terrors that lurked in the shadows. She glanced around, her eyes straining to see if there was anyone—or anything—watching her.

The street she walked down was, during the day, a writhing cauldron of activity, with hawkers and costermongers bellowing their wares at the masses of people bustling past them, crowds squeezed together in an attempt to keep from under the hooves of the horses charging by without care for who they rode over. As the light waned, the traffic on the streets was replaced with drunks and prostitutes, with the more respectable people choosing to travel in groups or, more likely, via some form of carriage: the faster moving the better. But there was rarely a time when the streets did not sing with some form of life, no matter how low.

However, on that late evening, these streets were preternaturally empty, as though everyone else had been called away. Everyone but her. It reminded her of that time, only a few years before, when the skies had ripped apart and the demons had streamed through from hell, terrorising London. They had been beaten back in part but, when the gateway to their hellish home had been closed, a fair number remained; some hunted down, others retreating into their own slum-like ghettos. For a moment she wondered if the reason for the emptiness of the streets was another demon incursion. But no: there was not enough noise for that. Demons were not known for their stealth. At least, not the demons that frequented London's streets.

Tap-tap.

Her worn-down heels beat a tattoo, the sound echoing off the dark, hollow buildings. She cursed the noise for giving her away, for making her loneliness even more acute. She toyed with the idea of removing her shoes and walking barefoot, but the thought didn't linger too long before being discarded: the ground was a fetid mixture of mud, faeces and all manner of broken items. She had seen other girls fall ill from the smallest cut, after getting infected from the muck coating the streets. It would be little comfort to escape the imaginary horrors around her by casting off her shoes and running home, only to die of God-knows-what, days later. And the stench would take weeks to scrub off her skin if she did live.

She shook her head. She was just imagining things, surely. She had walked these streets countless times in her life; no one knew them better than her. Every twist and turn was like an old friend, each stone or brick was as familiar as the lines on her own hands. There couldn't be anything there that she could ever be afraid of.

Tap-tap tap-tap.

It was too quiet, though; far too quiet. It felt as though the buildings around her were holding their breath, watching with horrified stillness for some unspeakable something to happen. To happen to her.

"Get ahold of yourself, Bessie," she said softly to herself.

"Your imagination's running away with you. Even London can be quiet sometimes."

The words sounded absurd even as they left her lips. London was never quiet. It was the noisiest hell-pit on Earth; a wonderful, chaotic, messy, beautiful sea of humanity. She could never imagine living anywhere else; she had never in her whole life strayed more than a handful of miles from the Bow Bells.

Tap-tap-tap-tap.

She had heard the rumours, of course. Rumours of a gang responsible for the sudden disappearances of girls all round the East End. A gang of men—or… something—which left no trace of their passing apart from fear and rumour.

She had heard the rumours but laughed them off. After all, hardly a week went by without another shadowy East End villain being talked of in hushed voices on street corners. If it wasn't Spring-Heeled Jack, it was Jack the Ripper. There were always men—and it *was* always men, let's face it—out there wanting to do harm to women. Half the time they were a real threat, half the time they were nothing more than fairy tales told to keep girls wary and safe indoors, away from all the bad things they could do if they were let out on the streets and to their own devices.

This gang was different, though: everyone said. There was not a soul in London not in fear of these new monsters. Even the demons feared them, went out in pairs for their own protection.

This new menace. Even their name sent a shiver down the spine.

The Tappers.

Tap-tap-tap-tap.

She picked up her pace, glancing around. She cursed herself under her breath, knowing she was letting her fears get the better of her, but unable to stop the relentless press of her fevered imagination.

Taptaptaptap. Taptaptaptap. Taptaptaptap.

She froze. While every inch of her being willed her to keep

3

moving, to get away from that place, she could not move.

She heard something behind her, a shuffling sound. Feet approaching her steadily from behind.

Slowly she turned. And screamed.

Chapter Two

Dicky Jones pulled his cap down over his face and the collars of his jacket up as he stepped onto Whitechapel High Street. He glanced up at the clock on the steeple of St Mary's and then cursed. Just after six o'clock; he was late for opening up. He shook his head as he started his march through the growing crowds, trying to force some life into his drowsy body. He blamed the demons; ever since they had expanded their ghetto to just one street behind his house, he had struggled to sleep.

In fact, ever since the demons had invaded from the Aether, a couple of years ago, things had been decidedly not right. It hadn't heralded the end of days, as the preachers had wailed, but neither had things returned to anything approaching normality, even after the uneasy truce had broken out, with the government choosing to ignore the new supernatural residents across the country as long as they didn't cause too much chaos. Dicky prided himself at being able to roll with the punches, to adapt to new times, and had managed to eke out a steady living by selling magical books and trinkets which might very well protect you against all things demonic, if you were lucky. But he drew the line at his sleep being disturbed by the supernatural noisily tearing each other to pieces just behind his house.

"Hey, you!"

Dicky glanced over his shoulder, squinting as he tried to peer through the massed bodies around him. Someone bumped his shoulder and he rounded on them, a curse on his lips, before he noticed the two men bearing down on him.

"Bugger." He turned and made his way in the opposite direction as quickly as he could, dodging left and then right as he made his tortuous way through the moving barricades caused by the sheer number of people filling the streets. It was already shaping up to be an unusually busy market day, and it seemed like everyone in the East End was out enjoying the promise of crisp early Spring sunshine as they hustled to make a living, haggled over food and wares, or went about altogether more sinister business.

Dicky had spent all his life on those streets and was used to the rhythm of the crowds, able to work the flow of bodies like an expert boatman, carving through them with ease when the need arose. However, at that moment sheer panic destroyed all those years of practice, leaving him as clumsy as a new-born.

"Out of my way!" he shouted, trying to force his way past a group of young men, who turned and glared at him, one man barging him aside into the path of another group. He tried to untangle himself, but it was too late. He looked up to see Spencer and Bart standing over him.

"Mornin', Dicky," grinned Spencer, a short, scrawny man with a face like a weasel and a voice to match. "Been a while. Mind if we have a chat? Didn't think so. Bart, help Dicky to his feet."

Dicky tried to back away as Bart's lumbering bulk lent down over him. His vision was filled with the man's excessively hairy body and completely smooth head as two hands the size of shovels grabbed him by the shoulders and hauled him—surprisingly gently—to his feet.

"This way," said Spencer. "Let's get away from all this noise, so we can hear ourselves speak, eh?"

Bart propelled him in the direction Spencer had indicated,

which Dicky noticed was the opposite way from where he had been heading. While he baulked at being dragged further away from the safety of his shop, he supposed that it could be a blessing; hopefully it meant that they did not have designs on damaging his property. This time, at least.

That still left the possibility that they planned to damage *him* though, he realised miserably, grunting as he was pushed against a wall.

"What do you want?" he asked when he got his breath back.

"Now, is that a way to greet old friends?" Spencer asked with mock dismay. "I'm hurt. Bart, are you hurt?"

"Very," rumbled Bart.

"You've not seen us in ages, and the first thing you do is try an' run from us. Then you're rude to our faces. That's just not nice."

Dicky frowned at them. "I heard you'd got mixed up with the demons, and then got banged up. Word was, you were either going to be hanged or deported."

Spencer shrugged. "And yet here we are. You know us: always lucky."

"I heard your luck ran out."

"You be careful who you listen to." Spencer wagged a stick-like finger at him, his nails caked in layers of black dirt.

"I'd heard—" started Dicky, but he was cut short by Bart's fist connecting firmly with his stomach. He doubled over, gasping for breath.

"I think you're misinterpret-at-in' the situation here, mate." Spencer bent down and spoke in his ear, his foul breath making Dicky gag. "We're not here to have a chat. We're here to talk *at* you. You see, you've let some people down, and they've sent us to collect."

Dicky sucked in a deep breath and pulled himself upright. He felt light-headed, the world seeming sharp and alien to him all of a sudden. None of what they were saying made any sense.

"Let people down?" he asked. "Who?"

"Come on," chided Spencer. "You know."

"Yeah," said Bart. "You know."

Dicky frowned. "No. I really don't."

"Yeah, you do," said Spencer.

Dicky opened his mouth, and then closed it and shook his head. "Why don't you remind me?"

"If we need to remind you," said Spencer slowly, "that means you've forgotten. And then our employers are goin' to be *really* unhappy with you."

"What employers?" Dicky asked. "Last I heard, the two of you were cut off; no one would work with you. The stuff you did, that's not the sort of thing people come back from."

"I told you," said Spencer through a thin smile. "We're lucky."

"No." Dicky grew in confidence as he spoke. "No one's that lucky. Not after all you did." He looked from one of them to the other, noticing the way they stared at him just a bit too hard, the tension in the way they stood, the desperation in their voices. "You're lying to me," he said slowly, the realisation making him giddy. "You've got some front, comin' here with your fairy tales of workin' for people who I've let down. Next you'll be telling me you're one of them Tappers, as well!"

Dicky's heart quickened as the other men flinched. Had he gone too far? He looked around, fearing that just the merest mention of the Tappers would be enough to conjure up those dreaded creatures from thin air. He shook himself; that was just the stuff of scare stories, surely.

"Point is, you can't tell me who you're workin' for or why," said Dicky. "And I know for a fact you're not a part of any gangs no more. You're on your own, so all these threats… You don't scare me."

He waited and watched them, his heart in his mouth as he half-expected a sudden fist to his face as reward for his words. His bravado started to seep away as he imagined them laying into him, beating and kicking him to within an inch of his life for daring to challenge them, these once-feared gangsters.

But they had always been feared more for who they ran with than for who they were, and Dicky knew that all of their friends had deserted them. At least, he hoped so.

Bart clenched and unclenched his fists, but he kept his eyes on his friend. Spencer took a halting step forward. "You'll regret this…"

"Why?" Dickie asked, emboldened even more by the fact that neither man had punched him yet. "What'll you do?"

"We'll…" Spencer shrugged. "You'll regret it, that's all."

Dicky looked from one to the other, lightheaded with relief that his instincts had stood him in good stead, for once. He let out a chuckle. "You're nothing," he said. "You're just a nuisance, both of you. Now leave me alone."

Bart stared at Spencer, who shook his head slowly. Dicky almost wondered if he could see tears in the other man's eyes.

*

Over in Stratford-upon-Avon, the mist rolled over the river, reaching out faint tendrils towards the banks and the church beyond. The gently flowing grey water seemed to deaden all sound, making the sobs and sniffles of those in the graveyard seem muffled and other-worldly.

Tessie stood by her parents' graves, trying to summon up some form of emotion. It had all happened so fast: they had gone from being the proud figures standing at her side on her wedding day to this, just two caskets being lowered into the ground. The two people who had brought her into this world, cared for her all her life, and now they were gone.

It was no use. Try as she might, she could not summon up any sorrow or grief or heartache, not even the slightest tear. There was a cold, empty hole where her heart should be. Did this mean that her mother had been right all along? Was she really just a broken thing, a shell only capable of redemption if she embraced a God which her scientific beliefs told her did not—could not—exist?

The clouds parted to let through a cold light. She looked to the heavens; the weather could at least have provided some sort of misery to match the occasion. Was a bit of rain really out of the question?

Her husband, the Honourable Lord Marchant, shuffled at her side, clearly impatient to get moving. *Good*, she thought. *Let him wait.* Not even *he* would be so callous as to pull her away from her parents' funeral. She relished that small sensation of power, one of the few times she had felt anything other than mute helplessness for a long time.

A parade of commiserating faces filed past, telling her how sorry they were for her loss. Empty words from empty people, who cared even less than she did.

All her life she had wanted to be free from her mother's stifling control, to be able to do what she wanted without being forced to idolise her spitefully judgmental God. Every step she took scrutinised. Always being measured against standards she would never, ever meet, no matter how hard she tried.

She had always wanted to be free from her mother, but not like this.

Marchant took her arm with a touch as gentle as a silken noose. She frowned up at him. He had claimed to be as upset as anyone at her parents' death, speaking at length about how good her mother had been to him. To hear him talk, one would have thought that *he* had been the one who had suffered the greatest loss.

Still, she thought coldly, *the fortune he had just come into as the husband of the only child of the two corpses being buried in the ground… That would dampen his pain ever so slightly, surely.*

He nodded at the people who were shuffling away, at the carriage which waited for them at the gates beyond. "Time to go," he said in a tone which almost approached gentleness. "If we want to make it back to London in time…"

Tessie sighed and gave him a half-nod. "I would like a few

more moments," she said. "Alone. Would you wait for me in the carriage?"

He frowned at her, his lips starting to part in a rebuke which was choked back as soon as he noticed the vicar watching them closely. With a curt nod, he turned and marched toward the gates. "Five minutes," he barked over his shoulder.

She pulled a face at his retreating back, and then blushed as she felt the vicar's eyes on her. "I am sorry," she said. "I suppose that is not the proper thing to do in a place like this."

He shrugged as he came to stand by her. "The Lord forgives many things of those who are grieving, or who find themselves in… difficult situations."

"I suppose so," she said softly. "So if He's responsible for all this, who forgives Him?"

"The Lord does not ask for forgiveness. The Lord forgives."

She shook her head. "I do not want His forgiveness. I do not want anyone's forgiveness. I just want…"

"What?"

"Nothing," she sighed. "Nothing at all."

*

"I still think we should have roughed him up just a little bit," said Bart as they watched Dicky walk back through the crowds. "That was just plain humiliatin'."

"No point," said Spencer. "Anyway, we got what we wanted: time. And here he is." He nodded towards Dicky's shop, at a tall man who was making his way casually towards them, his body slightly hunched to hide a bulk under his jacket.

"He did it!" hissed Bart, a slight touch of wonder in his voice.

"Of course he did," said Spencer. "But we did all the hard work; all he had to do was walk in there and take the stuff. Like I always say: he's nothin' special."

"But that's Seth," said Bart. "He's…"

"He's a hardman, I'll give you that. But he's still a crook

and a conman, just like you and me. If he was such an amazing criminal mastermind, he wouldn't have needed us to do this; he could've just marched in and told Dicky to give it to him."

Neither Seth nor Dicky—thief and victim—were aware of Spencer's scorn or Bart's muted admiration. They walked within mere feet of each other; Seth studiously ignored the other man, while Dicky was oblivious to anything except putting as much distance as he could between himself and the two men behind him. Preferably by getting back to his shop as soon as possible.

It felt to Spencer and Bart as though the whole market held its breath as Seth and Dicky passed each other, the others around them fading into the background as the only focus of their world became whether their colleague would make it back to them without being spotted.

Then something intruded into Spencer's field of vision: a young boy who could have been no older than seven or eight years of age. He was wandering aimlessly, clearly wanting to earn some coin by picking pockets but with no real idea of how to do it, or even the courage to try. As he watched, Spencer saw his younger self in that boy: a scrawny street rat abandoned by parents with more important things to do, and ignored by peers who didn't want to waste their time helping the runt of the litter.

The memories came flooding back, of running terrified through endless streets full of people so much taller than him, a forest of legs which battered and beat at him at every turn, stopping him from getting anywhere. He had spent his days constantly losing his friends, struggling to keep up with them as they skipped with ease through the moving obstacles which made up the streets of London's East End.

But then he had realised that his size could actually be his saviour. It made him invisible, and that realisation gave him power: he could skip around unnoticed, and disappear before anyone knew he was there. He was fast as well: being light and scrawny had its advantages.

He still remembered his father's words, the only gifts the man had ever really granted his son, in one of the rare moments when he wasn't drinking or sleeping. *"You've got to use the gifts you're given, lad. You're never going to be big and strong; you're never going to be able to stand up in a fight. But you can run, and that's your real strength. Any time you're faced with anything you can't talk your way out of, you run: as fast as you can. Remember that and you'll always be all right."*

The words came flooding back as he watched the tiny, scared kid bump and blunder through the crowds, oblivious to the group of larger children watching him with hungry grins. Spencer could not tell if those others were friends or kin or gang mates, or just plain predators. But he knew from painful experience exactly what was in store for the child.

The gang started to advance, picking their way toward the still blissfully unaware child, who was focused more on plucking up the courage to try lifting a purse from one of the passing trousers than watching around for potential dangers.

They drew nearer, fanning out in a horseshoe shape, slowly closing the trap to give their prey no chance of escape.

Spencer held his breath. He counted the gang: eight of them. More than he would be able to handle, although Bart's size alone would probably be enough to at least make them think twice.

Even while he was forming those thoughts, the jaws of the trap were closing even further around the child. Spencer remembered the beatings he had received in just such situations, his mind's eye conjuring up afresh the metallic taste of blood and the red hotness of being pounded into senselessness.

He couldn't let the boy suffer that same fate. He was small; why didn't he do the one thing he could do better than those larger kids? Why didn't he do what he needed to do?

Without thinking, Spencer shouted: "Run! You there: run!"

The market turned as one to face him. Stallholders and customers paused and glanced at the bellowing madman. The gang of children, surprised, stopped and stared, guilt written all over their reddening faces. The boy looked at him with wide eyes, then noticed the other children circling round him. In an instant, he had fled.

Dicky had also spun round at the sound of Spencer's voice, and as he did so he noticed the panicked fury on Seth's face, not more than a few feet away from him. "I know you…" he started. Then he noticed the bulk under the other man's jacket. "Hey!" he shouted, making the connection between Seth and the other two men.

Seth broke into a sprint, pausing for a split-second to glare at Spencer as he passed. "I'll deal with you later," he hissed before charging away.

Spencer and Bart looked at Dicky's rapidly approaching form, then at each other, and then burst into a run.

They weaved through the crowds of pedestrians and costermongers, coming a close cropper with a market stall and then again with a rather intransigent donkey. Reaching the end of the street, they turned right and then into a side street, ducking under lines of washing and around piles of rubbish. Barging through a door, they elbowed past a drunken man who had been roused by the racket created by their passage, emerging into a courtyard filled with screaming children, scowling women, and tubs half-full of tepid water.

Over a wall, through another courtyard and house, up some stairs, along a rickety roof, a short drop down to the street and then they ducked into an alley, squatting in the relative darkness to check whether they were still being followed.

After a few minutes they both relaxed and swaggered back into the street. "Where now?" asked Bart.

"The Crown," said Spencer. "To collect our end of what Seth took."

"You sure? He didn't look too happy when he ran past us."

"He'll be fine. It's business, ain't it?"

*

"You've got some nerve," growled Seth. "After you nearly cost us the whole job. What were you playing at back there?"

They had finally caught up with him in the Rose and Crown, a rundown, dark, narrow pub on Commercial Road in the heart of the East End: a place where *'Don't ask, don't tell'* was less a phrase and more a way of life. As a result it was beloved of thieves and other folk of dubious means; the landlord was so practised at maintaining secrets that many wondered if he really did have no memory at all.

Seth had taken up his usual spot, as far back in the room as possible, his chair facing the door. When Spencer and Bart had arrived, he had studiously ignored them until they were stood in front of him. On the table sat a large, bound red book, the edges of the pages yellowed and tattered. On its cover was a swirling devil motif.

"There was this boy…" started Spencer, already realising how weak his argument sounded. "He was in trouble…" He glanced at the bar, but Seth's intentions were clear: any drinks privileges they might have had were well and truly withdrawn.

"Some boy," said Seth slowly. "You nearly threw away this score because of *some boy*. Relative of yours, was he?"

"Well, no…"

"Did you even know him?"

"Not really, but… Look, what's the problem? You got the loot, didn't you?" Spencer nodded at the book on the table between them. "Is this it? Seems a lot of trouble for just a book."

"It's not just any book," said Seth. "Our client is paying a pretty penny for this. And you nearly blew it with that show out there." He looked up. "In fact, here he is now. You two, make yourselves scarce."

Spencer and Bart quickly stepped back to stand against the wall, trying to look as inconspicuous as they possibly could. Under normal circumstances, given the way they normally looked, this would have been a tall order. But in the shady surroundings of the Rose and Crown, they blended in perfectly.

They watched as a tall, dark man approached Seth's table. He was clearly very wealthy, his clothes alone costing more than most in the bar would see in their lifetimes. He wore a black coat over a black suit and carried a black cane topped with a silver skull, gripped in a black gloved hand. Ordinarily a lone person walking into somewhere like the Rose and Crown displaying their wealth so obviously would simply be a target for the hungry thieves which crowded around there. However, there was something about the man and his bearing which caused all those present to turn a blind eye to him, shrinking away from the dark power that seemed to seep from the man.

He removed his hat to reveal a head of immaculately groomed black hair and a long, thin face from which peered two piercing dark eyes.

Even Seth seemed to be wary of the man, standing hastily and wiping his hand on his trousers before offering it in greeting. The man looked at it, showing no intention of returning the gesture. Seth cleared his throat as he lowered his hand and then gestured to the table. "There's your book, sir."

The man swept it up from the table and shot Seth a cold glare. "This is the Grand Grimoire, one of the rarest and most dangerous texts in the known world. And yet you have it laying on a table in a public bar, in full view of all and sundry?"

"I'm sorry Mr Emerson, sir, I…"

"Do *not* use my name, especially not in here, of all places!"

Seth cast his eyes down, the picture of the subservient commoner being berated by his better. If he had had a cap in his hands, he would have been wringing it. Spencer found himself enjoying the spectacle as he watched from the shadows.

"Of course sir. Sorry."

The man—Mr Emerson—thumbed through the book. "However, you have delivered exactly what I ordered, and it all seems to be in order. Was there any trouble? You did not attract any attention?"

"No, none at all," said Seth quickly.

Mr Emerson stared at him for a long moment, as though he was peering into his soul. Spencer flattened himself further back against the wall, tensed and ready to run if the focus were to shift to him.

Mr Emerson nodded sharply. "Very well. The person you liberated it from will not have acquired it by legal means anyway, and such an item would be frowned on by the authorities, so there is no risk of the police getting involved." He tossed a brown purse on the table, which landed with a satisfyingly heavy clink. "There is your payment. You will find it all there. Do pass on my regards to your employer and thank him for a job well done. I am sure I will be in touch with further assignments in due course." He turned and marched out the door; as soon as he did so it was almost as though the pub, having held its breath since he had entered, suddenly breathed a sigh of relief. The sound of the customers and staff rose up once more, and the place seemed somehow lighter.

Spencer walked back over to the table, where Seth was counting through his payment. "That's a nice pay-out, right?"

Seth glared at him. "No thanks to you. But I suppose you did do some form of service, so here's your cut." He tossed a handful of coins across the table at them.

Spencer counted the coins. "Here, that's not fair! We did all the work distracting him—"

"And you damn near lost the whole score with that whole shouting palaver! You should be grateful to get even that."

"But—"

"But nothing. You're a liability, the pair of you. And don't try using your trained ape to try and threaten me. You want to make a complaint, take it up with Milton." He sneered at them. "I thought not. Not even you two are that stupid. Now get out my sight before I change my mind and take that money off you."

Spencer leant forward, trying to show a bit of steel in his manner, let down by the simple fact of how he looked. "You should know better than to treat us like this," he said, trying one final throw of the dice. "We've got connections, you know."

Seth stood up and both Spencer and Bart took a step back. They knew what he was capable of, even on his own.

"*Had* connections," corrected Seth. "As in, you used to; not anymore. You've got no protectors, no gang, no manor. Milton's only a short way from ordering both your throats cut. I only agreed to cut you in on this one as a favour, and you almost threw it all away for the sake of some kid. You're out of luck, Spencer. Both of you."

Chapter Three

The room's stillness was punctuated only by the clicking of needles and the tick-tock-tick-tock of clocks on the mantelpiece. Tessie was surrounded by dull, respectable neatness: from the dark furnishings to the sober rugs, from the refined window dressings to the chaste company within. The noise from the street outside was reduced to a distant clatter of the occasional hoofbeat and the muted yelling of costermongers. Within was a place of solitude and contemplation, where upstanding young ladies could occupy themselves in a respectable manner.

Tessie puffed out her cheeks and exhaled slowly, ignoring the disdainful glares prompted by the unladylike noise as she fiddled with the cloth in front of her. She had been at it for what felt like an eternity already, and all she had to show for her efforts was something which, if you looked at it hard enough, could maybe in some way hint at being something like a flower. She screwed up her eyes and squinted at it, her mind composing equations which could describe the vague shape she could see emerging. There, of course, was the problem: how could she focus on flowers and pretty colours when her mind was filled with much greater questions?

She knew without looking just how pristine and particular the other ladies' creations would be. She had never had much of a mind for creating such things. No imagination, her mother had always said, which was probably true. Give her a pattern to follow and she could copy it down to the smallest detail. But ask her to be creative and it was as though someone had poured ice-cold water all over her brain, freezing any thoughts before they could even start to congeal into something coherent and interesting.

She stared towards the window, watching the dust motes play in the afternoon light, imagining that each of them was a tiny fairy, willing and eager to grant her wishes. She allowed herself the shadow of a smile as she pictured herself turning into one of those fairy-motes, flitting up and dancing free, into the light and then through the window and up, up into the sky.

The fact was, she would rather be anywhere rather than in that stuffy room with those stuffy people. But *he* had insisted that she be there, and she could not be seen to disobey her husband.

She tutted, and forced herself to focus properly on her sewing once more, hoping that the rhythm of repeatedly stabbing something would take her mind off everything else. She pictured her husband's face as she did so.

"My dear," said a voice at her side. "This is supposed to be a process of relaxation and contemplation, not an exercise in blood-letting."

Tessie blushed as she glanced over at Margaret. The slightly older woman was regarding her with one eyebrow raised, but otherwise everything about her was as perfectly poised as always. They had only really known each other for a few months, ever since Tessie had moved down to London, but in each other they had recognised kindred spirits, each of them being more independent-minded than most other women in their social circle. Margaret had also been an acquaintance of Tessie's mother, and so had assumed responsibility to ensure she settled in her new home.

"I am sorry," Tessie said. "I do not know what came over me."

"Indeed," Margaret said. Tessie endured a few awkward

minutes' silence as she tried desperately to put on the pretence of being immersed in the activity before her, until the other lady finally sighed and leant over to talk.

"If you do not mind me saying," Margaret said in a conspiratorial half-whisper. "But you do seem rather out-of-sorts at the moment. Is anything amiss?"

Tessie shook her head, cursing her cheeks for flushing as she lied, "No, not at all."

Margaret tutted. "Come now, young lady. You cannot fool me. Out with it. Is it… marital in nature?"

Tessie's cheeks burned even more intensely. "I do not know what you mean."

Margaret regarded her. "It is not unusual for newly-married ladies, especially those on their first marriage, to find that the experience does not live up to the fairy tale they may have previously believed it to be."

Tessie tried not to bark a laugh at this. She had had such low expectations of marriage to begin with, that anything would have been considered an improvement. Although 'fairy tale' was far, far from all of that.

Mind you, even her lowest expectations did not hold a candle to the creeping sense of nameless dread and discomfort she felt on an almost daily basis. She would almost have preferred it if he did beat her: at least that way she would have had something to pin her fears to, something she could take action against. But this…

"I am sure you are right," she said, adopting the pose of the dutiful, penitent wife. "It was always too much to expect. And mother always says that I can be too flighty, with my head in the clouds most of the time."

Margaret nodded, satisfied, and returned to her needlecraft. "Things are never as bad as they may seem."

Chapter Four

Spencer and Bart prowled the streets heading away from Seven Dials, and in the general direction of Covent Garden. Bart occasionally glanced over at his friend, but otherwise kept quiet. Spencer, for his part, kept his head down, cheeks burning a bright red and fists clenched at his side.

After a while, Bart could stand the silence no longer. "So what now?" he asked.

Spencer shrugged. "I guess we're screwed," he sighed.

"Really? That's it? Ain't there anything we can do?"

Spencer stuck out his lower lip and frowned. "We could go and drink away our problems with what he's given us. Probably wouldn't be enough to get us properly trolleyed though. Thing is, he's right: without Milton we're nothing. We don't get no scraps from the table, and we don't get his protection either."

"Must be something we can do? You know, get back in his good books?"

Spencer shook his head. "Only thing folk like Milton respect is money. If people earn for him, then…" He turned and grinned at his friend. "Of course! We earn. We go back to the old ways, how we first made our names. Let's go and do some good old-fashioned grifting. When Milton sees what we're capable of, he'll have to let us back in. What do you reckon, mate? Fancy a bit of petty theft?"

Bart grinned back at him. "Thought you'd never ask."

*

They walked through the crowded piazza of Covent Garden, looking for all the world like two men casually strolling through on their way to work, while surreptitiously keeping an eye out for any marks worth stealing from.

"There," said Spencer through the side of his mouth. "Toff in the black tailcoat, with the bird in red."

"I see 'em," replied Bart. "You ready?"

"Let's do it."

They split up, Spencer circling round the back of the unsuspecting couple while Bart made a beeline straight for them. As he walked, Bart rolled his gait, bumping into people and snarling at any who were brave enough to protest. A buzz started to build around him, a pocket of people focused on this uncouth hulk of a man who seemed intent on causing trouble. It wasn't long before the couple Spencer had spotted were also drawn into the distraction, looking over at Bart and trying to figure out how they could avoid or ignore him without drawing his wrath.

Spencer popped up behind them, nimble fingers removing the man's pocketbook while he was focused on trying to keep his partner safe from the bustle around them. It was then that he noticed the two policemen making their way towards them. He whistled two short bursts of warning and then turned and melted into the crowd, Bart immediately following.

They made it to the edge of the piazza before being accosted.

"Oi, you two," bellowed one of the policemen. "Stop right there."

They both froze. "Should we try running for it?" asked Bart through the corner of his mouth.

"Not sure how far we'd get," said Spencer. "And they'd just

nick us for avoiding arrest. Just leave it with me." He turned with a broad smile. "Afternoon, officers. What can we do for you?"

"Spencer and Bart," said the policeman, a middle-aged man with a long, handlebar moustache. "It's been a while."

"Certainly has, Mr Jones. Been keeping ourselves out of trouble, just like you told us to."

"Why do I doubt that," PC Jones replied. "Come on, turn out your pockets."

"What? Why?"

"Because I'm pretty sure you've just lightened someone's pockets back there. That performance by your big mate was a blatant distraction if ever I saw one."

"I am shocked and disgusted," said Spencer. "Aren't you, Bart?"

"Totally. Comes to something when you can't even walk down the street without being accused of stuff."

PC Jones stepped forward. "Don't make me ask twice, boys. If you've not done anything, then you won't mind showing me what's in your pockets."

They stared at him for a moment and then shrugged. Bart went first, pulling out a handful of rocks and a half-eaten hunk of bread.

Spencer stared at him. "Really? I thought we'd stopped collecting rocks?"

"I liked the look of 'em," Bart shrugged. "Look: this one's got a nice pattern on it. Never know when you might need a nice rock."

"I can confidently say there's never been a time when I've needed a nice rock," said Spencer.

"What if it's a very expensive rock?" asked Bart. "Like a diamond."

"Any of them rocks in your hand very expensive?"

"Well, no. Found 'em on the floor, didn't I? But I like 'em."

Spencer shot an exasperated glance at the policemen. "I take it being in possession of random rubbish isn't a crime?"

"Not that stuff," said PC Jones. "But what about you?"

"I don't have any rocks," said Spencer.

PC Jones rolled his eyes. "Empty your pockets."

"Is this really necessary?" asked Spencer. "You see, I think this is just plain intimidation. That's what this is. You seen us do anything wrong?"

"I don't need to see you committing a crime to suspect you of one," replied the policeman. "I know you two. Now, empty your pockets or I'll arrest you and then empty them for you down the station. And I won't be gentle about it."

"All right, all right." Spencer turned his pockets inside-out. "See? Nothing there."

PC Jones gestured to his colleague, who stepped over to check, patting Spencer to check he wasn't keeping anything hidden elsewhere on his person.

"Very well," PC Jones said slowly. "But you two should know that we're keeping an eye on you. Step out of line just once, and you're straight to the nick. And after all the other times you've been in front of a judge, trust me when I say the next time will be your last. Either swinging from a noose or shipped off to some prison colony, you won't have a chance to bother anyone round here ever again. You understand?"

"Of course," said Spencer. "But we're reformed characters, see? You don't have to worry about us."

The policemen laughed. "Worried? We're not worried at all about you! But remember: you're being watched. All. The. Time."

The policemen walked away, and Spencer spat on the ground.

Bart turned to him. "Here, what did you do with the cash?"

"As soon as I saw the coppers, I knew we'd be pinched. I palmed it off on a couple of kids."

"Last we'll see of that, then."

"Better that than being nicked."

"Yeah, but… All of it? What about what Seth gave us? Not

that too?"

"That too."

"But we earned that, fair and square."

"By helping him nick that book. Not sure the coppers would've taken too kindly to that as an explanation, don't you?"

"S'pose not," grumbled Bart. "So what now?"

"Now? Well, now we're well and truly done for." He nodded over to the coppers, who were still watching them from the other side of the street. "Come on, we're going to get nothing from round here. I think we've still got some credit down at the King's Head. Let's drown our sorrows while we think of what to do next."

*

"Just who the hell do they think they are?" asked Spencer, slamming his jar of beer down on the table, ignoring the glances and glares from the rest of the pub.

"Well, they are the police…" said Bart.

"Yeah, but haven't they got better things to do than follow us around? Look: they're out there right now, still watching us! There are proper criminals out there, and what are they doing? Walking around after us like they're our shadows."

"I thought we *were* proper criminals?"

"Well, yes, but it's not like we're the really important ones, are we?"

"But you said…"

"I know what I said, but…" Spencer shook his head. "Look, let's face it, we've always been part of a crew, not the leaders. So why aren't they after them?"

"You mean blokes like Seth and Milton?"

"Yeah. And as for them, who do they think they are, bossing us around?"

"Isn't ordering people like us around… kind of what bosses are supposed to do? It's the sort of thing they've always done to us, ever since I can remember, anyway."

"Yeah, but there's ways and there's ways, you see?"

Bart shrugged and grunted noncommittally, clearly hoping that would be enough of a response.

Spencer carried on regardless. "You know what, this is all for the good. I'm sick of bein' treated like a slave, like a piece of dirt to be shuffled around whenever Milton wants. We spend all our lives running around at his beck-and-call, and for what? A few scraps from his table, that's all. And then he casts us away, without a by-your-leave."

"The thing is," Spencer continued, warming to his theme, "we've spent our whole lives running around doin' other peoples' bidding, getting nothing but trouble and little reward for our efforts. I think it's time we started properly earning our way in this world."

"You sure?" Bart looked from Spencer to his drink and back again, wondering if something had been dropped in the other man's beer. "That feels wrong, like it's kind of against the... what you call it—natural order—ain't it?"

Spencer glared at him. "Natural order? What do you know about *natural order*? Is it natural for us to spend all our time being bossed around, treated little better than kids or slaves? After all the years we've grifted for him, all the coin we've made him over the years, and this is how he treats us: like dogs. Worse than dogs: at least dogs get a roof over their heads and a meal now and again. He don't even give us that."

"Look," said Bart. "I know you're worked up about what just happened, but—"

"It's not just about that. This has been happening for a while now. After all the stuff we've gone through, all the times we've risked our necks. And now we've got the coppers crawling all over us."

Bart shrugged. "Cops have always been sniffing around us. They'll get bored soon enough."

"Maybe. But what do we do in the meantime? Time was, we

could rely on Milton to chuck us a few scraps to keep us going. Seth was pretty clear that ain't going to be happening again any time soon, wasn't he?"

"I suppose," muttered Bart, staring into his beer. "So what does that mean?"

Spencer shrugged. "Point is, we spent all our lives just following other people and got nothing to show for it but grief and struggle. I think it's time we change things round."

Bart toyed with his beer nervously. "Change? Why do we have to change stuff? I like things the way they are…"

Spencer shook his head. "Things will be better if we do stuff a bit different. You mark my words. If only to keep us away from the hangman's noose."

"All right…" said Bart slowly. "So what are you thinking?"

"We need to find something which will get us on the right path, a good earner which will set us up for life."

"You mean a big job? Like a train robbery or bank job?" said Bart, his eyes lighting up. Then he shook his head. "We don't have any leads into them sort of jobs. Not on our own. We'd need to get others involved. Then Seth'd just muscle in and take our share. Just like always. Just like you said you're trying to change."

Spencer took a long swig from his beer. "You're right. We need to break the cycle. We can't keep doing what we've always done, and anyway like you said we don't have the resources or connections. And with the cops sticking to us like this, one wrong step and we're done for." He stared down at his beer for a long moment and then looked up, a strange light in his eyes. "You know what I think we need to do?"

"What?"

"I think," Spencer said slowly, "that we need to go straight."

Bart laughed: a throaty, barking laugh which stopped as quickly as it had started when he saw the look on his friend's face. "You're serious, ain't you? But we don't know the first thing about goin' straight. We know less about goin' straight than we do about doing a big train job. What do we know about goin' straight?"

"How hard can it be? You just get a job and get paid."

"Sounds hard. And boring. We've always kind of worked for ourselves, kind of. What was it you always said? Folk who work for bosses in Civvie Street just end up working themselves to death, while their boss is the only one what gets rich?"

Spencer clapped his hands together. "And that's the thing! You see, that's the secret of goin' straight. Everyone takes from other people, that's how the whole thing works. But rather than waiting with your hand out for someone to give you a tiny share, if you work for yourself you can take the whole thing. And at the end of the day, all them toffs with their titles and taxes and jobs: that's just another name for stealing from other people, usually from the likes of us."

"You sure?" asked Bart slowly.

"Of course! They take from the likes of us by using up our time, working us to the bone so we make them nice clothes or look after their houses for them or make their food."

"Well, not really *us*, though," pointed out Bart. "We've never done any of that stuff, have we? We've kind of just nicked stuff all the time."

"That's not the point. What the toffs do is just stealing and grifting by another name. We've grifted all our lives, and got loads more experience of that sort of thing than any toff. We can play them at their own game and win, I guarantee it."

"All right…" said Bart slowly. "But what exactly would we do, then? Not sure there's much call for pickpockets or muscle in the legit world is there? Actually there could be call for muscle: we could protect toffs from getting robbed, couldn't we?"

Spencer shook his head slowly. "That sort of thing would just put us right against the likes of Milton, and we don't want to risk having to cross swords with any of our old mates, do we? If nothing else, it would just make him more likely to demand his cut from us. No, we need to do something which sets us against people we don't owe anything to. Or things."

"Things?" asked Bart.

Spencer grinned. "Yeah. I know exactly what we'll do. But first we're goin' to need some stuff to help us spread the word."

*

The apprentice wiped his eyes with his forearm as he shut up shop for the night. It was only recently that the proprietor, Mr Evans, had trusted him with the keys to the workplace and, while he was tired to his very bones, he still felt the tingle of excitement at the responsibility which had been bestowed upon him. He loved the feeling of being completely alone in the building, the master of everything around him. He stopped and turned, looking out over the huge hulking machine in the centre of the room. It was sleeping now, waiting for the morning when it would wake to create its magic once more. It was at moments like this he liked to imagine that his apprenticeship was over, and he was finally a Master himself: the pillar of society free to do whatever he chose with his own business.

He closed his eyes for a moment, lost in the daydream, and it was this pause that was to prove his undoing.

He turned at the sound of the door creaking open behind him. "Sorry, we're closed for the night," he said in a thin voice.

"Closed to customers, eh?" said a thin, weaselly-looking man as he stepped through the door. "That's all right. We're not what you call customers; more like friends. That's right, ain't it, Bart?"

The scrawny man stepped aside to reveal a much larger figure pretty much filling the doorframe. "Yeah," rumbled Bart as he stepped into the room.

"Friends?" said the apprentice doubtfully as he squinted at them. "Hang on, I recognise you two; you live on the same street as my folks."

"That's right. Friends: in fact we're practically family, ain't we?" Spencer clapped a bony hand on the apprentice's shoulder and steered him back into the room as Bart shut and bolted the door behind them.

"What do you want?" asked the apprentice, his heart pounding loudly. "We don't want any trouble here. My master, I'm sure he's paid everything he should—"

"Don't worry," said Spencer. "I'm sure everything is in order. We just came here to check out that everything was all right. And in particular to check that the quality of workmanship here is still as high as ever."

The apprentice blinked. "Quality? I can assure you that we take pride in our work. Mr Evans won't allow anything but the best to leave here. If you want to come back in the morning…"

Spencer walked over to the large machine. "So this is it, is it? This is the printer?"

The apprentice nodded slowly. "It's Mr Evans' pride and joy. Wait: don't touch—"

"Don't worry," said Spencer. "I'm not going to hurt it. But we'd be very interested in a demonstration, wouldn't we Bart?"

"We would." The big man's voice came directly behind the apprentice, making him jump.

"Well, if you'd care to come back in the morning, I'm sure Mr Evans would be more than happy to—"

"You see, the thing is," said Spencer. "We're not able to come back here in the morning. Got some important business to attend to, out-of-town. Ain't that right, Bart?"

"That's right."

"So we were thinking that it would be really neighbourly of you if you were to give us a bit of a demonstration right here and now. We'd be very, very grateful, if you know what I mean."

"Oh no," stammered the apprentice. "I can't possibly… I mean…"

"You do know how to work it, don't you?"

"Well, yes, of course—"

Spencer clapped the man on the shoulder. "Great stuff. Then prove it."

"What?" The apprentice stared at him as though he had just asked him to produce a donkey from his pocket.

"You heard. Prove to us that you know how to work it."

The apprentice's eyes flicked nervously from one man to the other. "But why would I want to do that? Why would I need to prove anything to you?"

Spencer sighed. "You see, the thing is, that my friend here has always wanted to see a proper printing press in action. Haven't you, Bart?"

"That's right," grunted Bart.

"And if he doesn't get to see one tonight, he's going to be very disappointed. Ain't you, Bart?"

"That's right."

Spencer put an arm around the apprentice's shoulder. "Do you want to know what happens when Bart gets disappointed?"

The apprentice stared wide-eyed at Bart, who was in the process of cracking his knuckles one-by-one. "N-n-no…" he stammered.

Spencer grinned. "Good man! So how's about you fire up the big machine and show us how it works? We won't take long; your boss will never know we've been here. Promise."

The apprentice started towards the machine and then turned back. "But what shall I print? I've put away the trays for the night, and there's nothing typeset at the moment."

Spencer shook his head. "Can't say I understand most of the words you just said there, but we've got something we'd love to see printed off all fancy, like. Show him, Bart."

Bart pulled a crumpled piece of paper from his pocket and unfolded it with great care, as though it was the most precious piece of paper in the world. He handed it reverently to the apprentice.

The apprentice stared at it. "You want me to print this?" he asked.

"That's right," said Spencer with a broad grin on his face. "Not too difficult, eh?"

"Well, no... Although it could do with a little--" The apprentice pulled a pencil from behind his ear.

"Don't you be messing with any of our words there, boy," snarled Spencer. "We have it just the way we want it. Makes perfect sense to us, don't it, Bart?"

"That's right," rumbled Bart, stepping towards the apprentice, who dropped his pencil in fear.

"But..."

"But nothing," said Spencer "Just you make sure it gets printed exactly as it's written down there, you understand?"

"Exactly like this?" asked the apprentice, holding the piece of paper in shaking hands.

"That's right," said Spencer. "Exactly like that."

"And what exactly do you want this printed on? Pamphlets? Posters?"

"Billboard posters. About a hundred should do it."

The apprentice stared down at the paper and then glanced uncertainly back at the two men. "A hundred copies exactly like this?" He shook his head and let out a long breath. "All right..."

Chapter Five

A few days later, Spencer and Bart sat in the corner of a darkened pub nursing two pints of beer, four tired legs and two bruised egos.

"I thought you said it'd get easier on the second day," muttered Bart.

"I know, I know," said Spencer through gritted teeth. "I just don't understand it. With everything going on right now, surely folks'd be champing at the bit to be rid of some demon problems. It's not like we're that expensive, ain't it?"

"Is it the posters? There something wrong with them?" asked Bart.

Spencer picked one up and studied it, then slammed it back down with a shake of his head. "Can't be. Although I did have to explain to a few folk what they said. That's the problem with them round here; most can't read."

"And most of them know us," pointed out Bart.

"Maybe that's the problem," mused Spencer. "I can see how people knowing our history might go against us, even though surely everyone knows there's no one better placed than us to deal with demons."

"Yeah, but doing jobs for the demons as a way of stoppin' them killing us—" at Spencer's glare, Bart quickly corrected himself, "—I mean, earning a bit on the side thanks to the demons, that ain't the same as huntin' them. At least, that's what a few guys said to me. After they finished laughin' at me, anyways." Bart muttered this last part into his ale before taking another long swig.

They glanced up as the landlord came over to collect the empty glasses from their table. "What's got you two so down in the dumps, then?" he asked.

"New business venture," said Spencer, waving at the pile of pamphlets in front of him. "Just taking a while to get going, that's all."

The landlord picked up one of the posters and studied it. "Demon hunting agency. I like what you've done with these posters. Nice name, too. 'Great Demon Hunting Agency' has a nice ring to it."

Spencer grinned triumphantly. "Great *Big* Demon Hunting Agency," he pointed out. "See, it works on two different levels: makes us sound like some big get-up, and also tells them we can get rid of any problem no matter how big it is."

"Nice," said the landlord. "Very clever. Had any nibbles yet?"

Bart shook his head. "Not a sausage. Just had people laughin' at me all day long. It was all I could do not to bang some heads together, but this one," he gestured at Spencer, "says that sort of thing's bad for business. Don't know about that, but it'd make me feel a lot better, and probably teach them a lesson to boot."

"It's early days," cut in Spencer, glaring at his friend. "We've got the know-how; no one knows more about demons than us two, right?"

Bart muttered darkly while the landlord glanced from one to the other, a doubtful expression on his face. He started to say something and then stopped himself.

"So, you got any demon problems you need a hand with?" asked Spencer.

"Actually," said the landlord, "I know old Bessie's had problems with some demons scaring off customers. You could try her. She might not pay that much, but she knows a lot of folk: you do a good job for her, she'd make sure plenty know about it."

Spencer grimaced. "I don't know…"

"Come on," said Bart. "You said we had to get work somehow. This is the first sniff we've had."

"Yeah, but…"

"What's his problem?" asked the landlord.

"Him and Bessie got history," grinned Bart. "Let's just say, last time they met, they didn't part on the best of terms." He nudged his friend. "Look at it this way: as well as getting some work, this might get you back in her good books."

Spencer scowled at them both. "Fine. But you can do all the talking on this one."

Bart downed the rest of his drink. "Good man," he belched. "Let's go."

*

They found Bessie on her usual patch, just by Seven Dials. The afternoon traffic of traders and pickpockets was starting to thin, to be replaced with the evening traffic of drunkards and muggers. She glared at them as they approached. "I'm working, boys. Go away."

"We're here to help you," said Bart. "We heard you was having some trouble. Demons and the like."

"And?"

"And we've set up a new business, helping folk who might be having trouble with demons. See?" He held up one of the posters.

"You know I'm about as much use with letters as you are, Bart," she said, baring uneven black teeth at him. "And what's he doing here."

"He's my associate, you know that."

"Yeah, well he's not welcome here."

"Fine by me," muttered Spencer, turning to go.

Bart stopped him, grabbing him by the arm. "We're a team, the two of us. You hire me, you hire him too."

"Wasn't aware I was hiring anybody," she said. "What would I want of you?"

"Like I said, we heard you was having some sort of demon problems."

She looked around and shushed him. "Keep your noise down. That stuff's bad for business. There are punters all round here: don't scare them off!"

"All right," said Spencer. "If you don't want our help then we'll just be on our way. Come on, Bart."

"No, no," she said. "Don't be too hasty." She lowered her voice. "You said you help with…?" she asked, then mouthing the words "demon problems".

"That's right," said Bart. "Bloke in pub said you were having some trouble. Suggested we speak to you."

"Well, you know…" she said, chewing her lip.

"Hang on," said Spencer. "Before you go any further, we only deal with demons. If it's the Tappers you're having trouble with, you're on your own."

She raised her eyebrows. "You surprise me, Spencer. Didn't have you figured for someone who believed in fairy tales and scare stories."

"You mean you don't believe in the Tappers?" asked Bart. "I've heard…"

"You've heard, we've all heard," she said, bobbing her head. "Thing is, I've seen more than my fair share of them things. Rippers and Spring-Heeled Jacks and all sorts of nonsense. And every time, they've not touched me. But the demons, now they're a different matter. One demon in particular. Every night it's the same: he's there, watching me, getting in the way of me earning."

Spencer chuckled. "Taken a shine to you, has it?"

She turned and stepped towards him, hand raised as though she was about to slap him. Then she deflated. "I don't know. But it's not good for business. I can't carry on like this. Can you help me?"

Before Spencer could say anything, Bart chipped in. "'Course we can."

*

They stood on the corner, watching as Bessie walked up and down the street, grinning and whistling at men as they passed. It didn't take long before they noticed a movement at the far end of the street. A very large movement.

"That the one, you think?" asked Bart.

"Looks like it," Spencer replied. "Big bugger, ain't he?"

"Bigger than I thought," Bart said. "But what's it they say about the bigger they are? Quicker they drop or something?"

"Something like that." Spencer looked around and then cursed.

"What's the matter?" asked Bart.

Spencer nodded over at the far end of the street, the opposite direction from where the demon stood. "Them bloody policemen, watching us."

"That a problem? Should we pull out?"

"Nah." Spencer shook his head. "We're not doing anything wrong here. If anything, we're doing their job for them." He turned back to look at the demon. "Any idea how we sort out that thing?"

"Was wondering if we just, you know, talk to him?"

Spencer laughed. "Talk to him?"

"Yeah. You know: tell him what damage he's doing. Maybe he'll…"

"What? See the error of his ways? You met many demons? How many of them been burdened with a conscience, you reckon?"

Bart shrugged. "First time for everything. Anyway, you got any better ideas?"

Spencer puffed out his cheeks. "I suppose not. Well, if it was one of them that are intent on just killing and stuff, it wouldn't be just hanging round on the corner every night. Come on then: let's give it a try."

They walked over to where the demon stood, trying to give off more confidence than they felt. The creature stood there, impassive and unmoving, to the extent that Spencer began to wonder if it wasn't in fact a statue. Then, as they stopped in front of it, it looked down at them, its huge slab of a head tilting slowly.

It stood over seven feet tall and seemed to have been etched out of solid stone. It was broadly humanoid in appearance, with arms and legs as wide as a grown man. Its body was wrapped in a rough red leathery armour which did not leave much of its body to the imagination. The head could have been mistaken for a helmet, shaped around two horns which stretched to either side, with two red pricks of light for eyes and a mouth full of sharp pointed teeth.

Bart looked at Spencer, who looked back at him. "It's your idea," hissed Spencer. "You go for it!"

Bart cleared his throat and looked up at the creature. "Evening," he croaked. "Wondering if we could have a word?"

The creature stared back down at him.

"Thing is," said Bart, "our friend there's noticed you watching her from time to time, and she's worried that you're damaging her trade, if you know what I mean?"

The demon continued to stare at him.

Bart glanced at Spencer and then licked his lips. "Um, could you...?"

Spencer stepped forward. "Look, do you understand us? Could you, very kindly, go away, and leave that lovely lady to work in peace?"

The demon stared for a moment longer and then swung a massive paw at Spencer. He ducked, but not quickly enough, and was caught a glancing blow across his chest which sent him flying, landing painfully against a wall on the other side of the street. It lumbered after him, massive feet making deep ruts in the muddy road.

"Oi, you, leave him," yelled Bart, running round to stand in its way. "Pick on someone your own size!"

It looked down at him and then its fist plummeted down towards Bart's head. Bart raised his hands above his head, catching the fist—just—before it beat down on his head. The demon looked at him, surprised that such a puny creature was able to withstand its power. Then it thrust its other fist out, punching Bart hard in the stomach and sending him flying, to land sprawled next to Spencer's groaning form.

The demon started towards them again, eyes glowing fiercely.

"Leave them alone!" Bessie ran over, throwing stones and whatever else she could lay her hands on.

"Yeah, leave 'em!" another girl joined in, followed by another and another. Soon there was a mob advancing on the creature. It looked around and then turned and stamped off.

Bessie ran over to the two groaning men. "That was probably the bravest thing I've ever seen," she said.

"Really?" asked Bart, wincing as he pulled himself up onto his elbows.

"Stupidest thing I've ever done," moaned Spencer. "I think I've broken something." He looked up and around. "Did we win?"

"We chased it off," said Bessie. "But you two stood up to it first. Showed us all we didn't have to be afraid of it. Maybe you're not so bad after all."

"Thanks," said Spencer. "Not sure it was worth it, but…"

"I'd say it was," said Bessie. She put her hand down her top and pulled out a grimy purse. She counted out a handful of coins. "It's not much, but it's all I can afford at the moment. Unless you'd like me to pay you some other way…"

Bart scratched his head, but Spencer quickly cut in. "That's all right. We'll take the cash, with thanks."

"I can help you some other way," she said. "I know people." She looked up. "Oi, Mungo, come here."

A grimy, wiry man wearing a suit two sizes too small for him walked over. "Yeah?"

"These two might be able to help you with that little problem of yours, eh?"

He scratched his chin. "Maybe. I think you might be right. What you reckon, lads? Fancy earning a bit more coin?"

Spencer sat up and then gasped in pain. "Yep," he grunted. "Always happy to help. Although if you could give us a few minutes to pull ourselves together?"

*

They crouched behind a low brick wall, watching as the demon stalked to and fro in front of the door to a large, battered old building. It was a smaller creature than the one they had just saved Bessie from, but still taller and bulkier than most men. Its skin was covered in scales and sores which were weeping green puss.

"I'm really not sure this is such a good idea," said Spencer. "Maybe we should just cut our losses while we still can. You know, while we still have all our limbs and can more or less walk away."

"Nah," said Bart. "This is fun. And we're getting paid. That's the dream, ain't it?"

"I suppose," muttered Spencer. "Now let's think: what did we learn from the last one?"

"Talkin' don't work," said Bart, holding up a thick length of pipe. "Get in and hit 'em first."

"Yes. And don't stand so close that they can hit you."

"Great. Then let's do this." Bart leapt up and started running before Spencer could raise a word in protest.

Spencer watched him run and cursed under his breath. "One day, he's actually going to listen to me," he muttered. "'Course, that's if we both live long enough."

Bart ran at the creature and swung the pipe at its head, hitting it with a satisfying ringing sound. The creature staggered back, and Spencer followed up with a blow of his own with a thick length of wood which shattered on impact. Bart was back in, swinging the pipe once, twice, three more times.

The demon dropped to one knee and then turned its head, looking up at them. Even though the creature's features were alien to them, they could recognise the look of exasperation and pure hatred it shot at them. "You two. You are dead," it hissed.

"Bugger," said Spencer. Then, turning to Bart, he yelled, "Run!"

Bart threw his pipe at the demon's head and then the two of them sprinted away, winding through the narrow streets and alleys, the demon hot on their heels. They turned left, right, left again, through a courtyard, over wall after wall, through hedges, until eventually they were able to stop and catch their breath.

"We lost it?" panted Bart.

"Shh!" Spencer held up a finger and listened. "I think so. Give it a few minutes and then let's go and find Mungo, get our money."

"You reckon it's been away from that door long enough for him to get in and out?"

"Don't know, don't care. We did our bit." He ran his hand across his brow, wiping the sweat on his trousers. "Bloody hell, there must be an easier way to earn money!"

A hand on his shoulder made him jump. "What on earth are you two up to?"

They looked up to see the two policemen standing over them. "Evenin', officers," Spencer managed, in between fighting to regain his breath.

"I thought we warned you…" began PC Jones.

Spencer held up a hand. "Now hold on, just wait a moment. We're not up to anything dodgy."

The policeman raised an eyebrow. "Why do we find that hard

to believe?"

"Honest! We've gone straight, just like you wanted us to. We're doing legitimate work and everythin'!"

"In my experience, two men running through the streets at night are engaged in anything *but* legitimate work."

"It's true," said Bart. "We're helping a bloke who was having some demon problems."

"Exactly," continued Spencer. "So unless there's a law against pestering demons—and last time I checked there wasn't—then you can't do us, right?"

PC Jones glared at them and then shrugged. "Just remember: we're keeping an eye on you." The two policemen turned and walked off.

Spencer puffed out his cheeks, then muttered a less than complementary word to their backs. "Come on," he said to Bart. "Let's go and collect our money, and then let's see who else needs our help."

Chapter Six

Mr Johnson, purveyor of fine foods and delicacies, warily eyed the two scruffy individuals who had just walked into his coffee shop. He nodded to his colleague, Mr Benson, who clearly shared his concern at the impact of these two newcomers to their shop's reputation as a high-class establishment. Mr Johnson put down his dishcloth and slowly but purposefully walked towards the two ruffians.

"May I help you, gentlemen?" he asked in a quiet voice.

The smaller, scrawnier one of the two nodded, taking off his hat almost deferentially and fingering what was left of the battered brim with grimy, mud-stained fingers. "Yeah you can, as a matter of fact. We are looking for the boss here: Mr Johnson. He about?"

Mr Johnson frowned. "That's me," he said. "How can I help you? Maybe we could chat outside?"

"We'll chat wherever suits you best, Guv," said the scrawny man. "We were sent here by a friend of yours, name of Jim Smith. Take it you know him?"

Mr Johnson sighed inwardly. That explained it: another of Jim's ne'er-do-wells, sent his way for yet another handout, simply to get them out of Jim's hair. When would this end?

"I know Jim," he said slowly. "What did he send you to ask

for from me?"

"Oh no," said the scrawny man. "He didn't send us to ask for anything *from* you; it's more what we can do *for* you."

"I'm afraid I don't follow," said Mr Johnson.

"You see, Jim tells us you have a bit of a problem that needs handling, something needing expert professional attention, if you get my meaning?"

"Not sure I do," frowned Mr Johnson. "Look, if this is just some convoluted way of menacing money out of me, wouldn't it be a lot easier and quicker for all of us if you just come out and say it?"

"Never fear," said the scrawny man, holding up a flyer in front of Mr Johnson's face. "My name is Spencer, this here's my associate, Bart. We're here representing the Great Big Demon Hunting Agency. Jim said you've got a problem we can help you with. You know, a demon problem." He tapped his nose conspiratorially.

Mr Johnson glanced around the room, suddenly aware of the interested glances they were receiving from the tables around them. The more superstitious of his customers had become more and more nervous, particularly given all the rumours of the mysterious so-called Tappers. Any suggestion that he was in any way connected to anything demonic would be very bad for business. "This way." He ushered the two men over to a table in the corner of the room. Spencer dumped the pile of posters on the table between them and stared expectantly at him.

"What exactly did he tell you?" hissed Mr Johnson.

"Just that you've been having a bit of demon trouble and could do with some help in a professional capacity, if you know what I mean," said Spencer, waggling his eyebrows.

Mr Johnson clenched and unclenched his jaw, his eyes darting around frantically as he checked to make sure that no one was listening in on their conversation. "That's not the sort of thing an establishment like ours would ever admit to, you understand?"

45

"No," frowned Bart.

Spencer shot his friend a glare. "We understand perfectly, squire. Total discretion is guaranteed every time. We are professionals, see?"

Mr Johnson eyed them up dubiously. "What sort of experience do you two have?"

"We've lived in the East End all our lives," said Spencer. "We were there when them demon portals started opening all over the place. We've been knee-deep in demons for as long as we can remember. We know all the tricks, and we know exactly how to deal with them. Hire us and, in no time at all, it'll be like you never set eyes on a demon at all."

Mr Johnson picked up one of the posters and studied it, his brow furrowed in thought. "My mother always told me never to judge a book by its cover," he said slowly. "And you say that Jim sent you to help me?"

Spencer nodded. "Yeah. Us and Jim go way back; helped him out of a few sticky situations. He ever tell you about the trouble he had with them gang-masters years ago?" He sat back and grinned, spreading his arms wide.

Mr Johnson raised his eyebrows. "That was you? Well, if you're capable of fixing a problem like that, then I'm sure you're capable of helping me with this one. How much?"

"Seeing as you're a mate of Jim's, how about we call it ten bob?"

Mr Johnson frowned. "That feels a bit steep to me…"

Spencer shrugged and stood up. "Well, if you'd rather not then I suppose we'll just leave you to it. I'm sure you'll find another way to deal with your problem." He started to raise his voice, prompting glances from the patrons seated around them.

Mr Johnson shushed him and waved him to sit back down. "What do you think you're doing?" he hissed. "I don't want anyone getting scared off by—" Then he nodded, realisation spreading across his face. "Very well. Ten bob it is. But you only get paid after you've done the job"

"Half now, half when we're done," said Spencer, his hand outstretched.

"I'll give you two now and the balance when you have performed your task to my satisfaction," said Mr Johnson. "That's my final offer. Take it or leave it."

Spencer slapped his hand into Mr Johnson's and shook it vigorously. "Then we'll take it," he said. "Now, tell us more about this problem of yours and we'll see what we can do…"

*

For Tessie, something even worse than sitting around in stuffy rooms pretending to be interested in sticking needles and thread into bits of fabric, was being forced to play the role of the dutiful wife, accompanying her husband on trips out of the house.

As they entered the coffee shop, her eyes lit up as she glanced around eagerly, hoping for some form of company, something to give her a few moments of relief from the drudgery of stilted conversation with her husband.

Marchant strode ahead of her, casting his imperious eye over the establishment and tutting as he noticed that his favourite table was occupied. Tessie took a quick breath and clenched her fists; she hated it when he got into petty rows just so he could belittle other people. Although she supposed it was a small blessing if the belittling was aimed at someone other than her.

Just as Marchant was about to make his way towards the table, his gaze flicked over to the proprietor, Mr Johnson, who was sat in deep conversation with two rather rough-looking fellows. Attracted by the sight of this much better sport, Marchant turned and walked over to them.

"Lord Marchant," said Mr Johnson, hurriedly scraping back his chair and rising to his feet. "Such a pleasure to see you again. I am afraid your usual table is currently occupied but I will make sure that that is rectified as soon as possible." He gestured rapidly to one of his serving staff, who quickly darted over to the table by the window to speak to the occupants.

Marchant nodded and picked up one of the posters lying on the table. "What do we have here, eh?" He said with a sneer in his voice.

"Nothing at all to bother yourself with, sir," said Mr Johnson, rapidly. He reached for the poster in Marchant's hands, but it was snatched away before he could retrieve it.

"Oh, I don't know. This does look rather amusing. I'm assuming this is some sort of joke?"

"No," said one of the ruffians still seated at the table, a rather short and scrawny-looking man.

Mr Johnson laughed nervously. "Yes, of course. In fact, these gentlemen were just leaving... Weren't you?"

"Yeah," said the scrawny man, glaring at Marchant. His companion stood as well, a mountain of a man who had not taken his eyes off Tessie since they approached the table. She found herself shifting uncomfortably under his gaze.

The two men gathered up the posters, with the exception of the one still in Marchant's hand, and started towards the door.

"Oh, by the by," said Marchant, holding out a hand to stop the two men. "I've heard of many sorts of demons but never a 'grate demon'. Pray tell me what exactly that is?"

"What do you mean?" asked the scrawny man.

Marchant waved the poster in the man's face, much to Mr Johnson's growing embarrassment. "This, on this poster. What is it?"

"That's the name of our agency," said the scrawny man. "The Great Big Demon Hunting Agency. It tells you what we do, see? We hunt demons, no matter how big."

"Yes," said Marchant, a wicked, teasing smile on his face. "But this 'grate demon' of which you speak: is it something which specifically dwells in fire grates, or does it sometimes venture out to spread soot on the carpets? On the rug? Is it a particular terror for housemaids and chimneysweeps?"

"I don't follow you," said the man.

"You spelt it wrong," muttered Mr Johnson.

"What? No we didn't. We meant 'great' as in 'big'."

"Yes," explained Mr Johnson patiently. "But what you wrote here was G-R-A-T-E: as in a fire grate. Not G-R-E-A-T as in, well, great…"

"Never mind, gentlemen," said Marchant. "I suppose you don't need little things like spelling or education to do what you do, eh?" He pressed the poster into Spencer's chest and walked over to his now-vacated table. Tessie followed him after a brief, apologetic smile to the two men and a curious glance at the poster.

*

The evening sun was a distant memory when the last of Mr Johnson's customers left his premises, leaving him to count his takings and shut up shop in the half-light cast by the candles scattered around the room. He looked up as the bell sounded to signify the door being opened once more. "I'm afraid we're closed for the night," he said without looking up. "If you care to come again in the—"

"Oh, don't worry about us needing any refreshments or the like," rumbled a deep voice from the doorway as the door was shut firmly. "We're not here for any of that; just our usual take."

Mr Johnson winced as he looked up to see the two burly demons towering over him. Both were much, much larger than even the tallest person Mr Johnson knew, with sharp, angular features, blazing red eyes, all topped off with visiting horns on the top of their skulls.

"We have come to collect our tribute," said the larger of the two demons. "You've got the usual ready for us?"

Mr Johnson looked around, nervously. "No."

The two demons looked at each other, evil grins playing across their faces. "Oh good," said the other beast. "It's so boring when people just give us what we want. It's a lot more fun when we have to rip it from their cold, dead hands. Literally."

Mr Johnson took a step backwards as the demon started towards him, just as Spencer cleared his throat from the other side of the room.

"I don't think you'll be doing that," said Spencer. "You see, this bloke here is under our protection now."

"And who might you be?" asked the larger Demon.

"I'm Spencer," he said. "You may have heard of me. I'm under the vassalage of Balrez."

The demon stared at him for a moment and then burst out laughing. "Yeah, we've heard of you," it said. "You're the lunch that Balrez lost. We were wondering where you got to."

Spencer spluttered in indignation as Mr Johnson stifled a terrified chuckle. "Lunch? What do you mean, *lunch*?"

"You were useful to him for a short period of time," leered the demon. "But you should know one thing about demons: if you're not useful to us, then you're food."

Spencer's eyes flickered from left to right, licking his lips nervously as the reality of his situation seemed to dawn on him. He backed away as the demons advanced on him, allowing Mr Johnson to sneak away to a back room unnoticed.

"Maybe we could talk about this, eh, gents?" stammered Spencer. "I could buy you a drink, we'll discuss this man to, erm, demon…?"

"The only thing we'll be drinking is your blood," rumbled the bigger demon. "Using your head as a cup."

Spencer made a dash straight through the centre of the two demons, narrowly avoiding the claws which grasped for him. He ducked underneath the savage-looking talons and then, after a brief stumble, found his footing and made for a door leading to the rear of the shop. He half-ran half-fell in his haste to escape the lumbering creatures close behind him.

He ran through the door and then slammed into the wall opposite. The door was narrow enough that the demons could only follow one at a time, with the faster--and larger--of the two reaching the door first. The demon ploughed through it, taking a large chunk of the masonry with it in its haste to catch its prey. No sooner had it made its way through the doorway when there was a flash of muddy silver and the demon's head flew from its body in an arc of blood. The body continued its forward momentum for a few moments, seemingly unaware of its sudden loss. Spencer backed away from the dismembered body, his eyes wide as he shouted at Bart, "Get this thing away from me! Bart, do something!"

Bart hefted his axe, ready for another blow, but then the body finally succumbed to reality and fell down to its knees, and then flat on its front with a loud crash.

The other demon crashed through the doorway, unable to arrest its forward momentum in time. The creature stared at the bloody scene in the room and, before it could react, Bart swung his axe again, this time at the creature's knees, taking one leg clean off and embedding the blade in the other. The creature fell to the ground, right next to the lifeless head of its comrade. Bart strode over and, putting one foot on the demon's body to brace himself, wrenched the axe free, ignoring the creature's howls of pain.

"That's a bloody good axe, that is," he said, admiring it.

The demon's howls turned into roars of anger as it tried to claw its way up onto its one good leg. "You have no idea what you've just done," it snarled. "I'm going to—"

"Bart, me old mate," said Spencer. "Do us a favour and take the other leg from him? Before he tries to do anything stupid."

"Be my pleasure, mate," muttered Bart, swinging the axe and sending the other leg flying in the opposite direction.

The demon roared even louder, the howls loud enough to wake the dead. Spencer knelt down next to the creature, close enough to speak to it without risking being within reach of the vicious claws that scrabbled around blindly.

"All right mate," said Spencer in a soothing voice. "Just calm it down, it's going to be all right." When the creature had dropped

51

its noise enough to allow him to be heard, Spencer continued. "Now you see, as I was saying, you and your kind don't have any say here no more. So you go and send that message back to all your demon mates, you hear?"

The demon laughed. "You're stupid as well as ugly," it snarled. "We'll send more of us here. We'll hunt you down and kill you. We'll—"

Spencer tutted. "And here was me trying to be all civil and polite. All I wanted you to do was the right thing and pass on a message for us, but now you've got me worrying that your heart just wouldn't be in it."

"He's right though, you know," said Bart. "Demons don't tend to take that sort of message well, do they?"

"Good point," mused Spencer. "In that case, we'll just have to do it ourselves." He waved a hand and stood up. "Do us a favour and take his head off for me?"

Bart grunted and, before the demon even had chance to shout a protest, the axe fell, cutting short the creature's bellow.

Spencer opened the back door and shouted, "You can come back in now. It's all over." He turned and grinned at Bart. "Well I think that went rather well, don't you?"

The door behind him opened a crack and Mr Johnston's nose emerged. "Is it really safe?" The man asked. "Are they… You know…?"

"Yes," grinned Spencer, pushing the door open wide. "All dealt with: see?" He gestured to the scene before them.

Mr Johnson gaped. "What have you done? Look at all this mess. You've…"

"We've dealt with it is what it is," said Spencer. He held out his hand. "I will be taking our payment now, as agreed."

Mr Johnson studied him. "Are you insane? I asked you to help deal with my situation, to stop me being harassed by these creatures. You've just started a war!"

"Don't worry," soothed Spencer. "You see, the thing about these demons is they never understand negotiations or talking or suchlike. You try and threaten or barter with these guys, they just come back for more and more. Won't respect you, see? Whereas this," he gestured to the two bodies, "is something they *will* understand and listen to. It's like two blokes having a pee and sizing each other up. We've just shown them who's got the biggest dick. Us. And we will be taking these heads and leaving them as an appropriate message in the appropriate place, won't we Bart?"

Bart grunted and stooped down to pick up the head nearest to him.

Mr Johnson put his hands up to his head. "No."

Bart paused, mid-stoop, as Spencer turned slowly to face the other man. "No? What d'you mean, 'no'?"

"I mean," said Mr Johnson, rubbing his temples with his thumbs, "that I will not pay you. As far as I can tell, you've fixed nothing; you've simply given me another set of problems. When I have seen that there will be no reprisals from these creatures'… confederates… then I will pay you."

"We had a deal," protested Spencer.

"Well, I am renegotiating that deal."

Spencer exchanged a glance with Bart and then tutted, putting an arm around Mr Johnson's shoulder. "When we first met, you struck me as a sensible sort of bloke," he said. "Seems like I might have to rethink that."

Mr Johnson blinked. "What do you mean?"

"I mean," said Spencer, "that you've decided that your most sensible strategy is to renegotiate with two blokes in possession of an axe."

"A bloody big axe," rumbled Bart.

"My colleague is correct," nodded Spencer. "Two blokes with a bloody big axe, which they've just used to kill two bloody big demons. And you fancy negotiating with us?"

Mr Johnson looked from one to the other and then reluctantly nodded. "All right. You win." He reached into his jacket and, pulling out his pocketbook, started to count out money.

Spencer licked his lips. "Actually, you know, you were right. We should renegotiate the contract. We'll take double."

"But you can't—"

"Actually, we can. On account of how you just tried to stiff us. Trust is gone, you see. Or would you rather we just left the demons here, heads an' all?"

Chapter Seven

Tessie jumped as the front door banged shut. He was back again. She forced herself to focus on her book, trying to make sense of what were now just shapes on the page. She fixed her gaze on just one word, pretending to be avidly reading, if only to give her a reason to not speak to him if he did enter the room, and then hopefully he would just leave her alone.

Her heart sank as the door opened and Marchant stalked in. After a moment's pause, where Tessie could feel his eyes boring into her, he walked over and sat in the wing chair opposite her.

She tried to force her breaths to come slowly and steadily, gritting her teeth in the vain hope that that would stop her heart beating so hard and her cheeks reddening so much.

After a long pause, Marchant cleared his throat. "A good book, is it?"

She made a show of deliberately marking her place and closing the book. Then, placing it on the side table next to her chair, she looked up and fixed her face into the best impression of a pleasant smile that she could manage. "Yes, thank you, it is."

He stared at her, impassive. After a few moments she could stand the silence between them no longer and asked, "How has your day been, husband?"

"Pleasant enough." He examined his nails. "I met with my

associates this morning. One of them will be joining us for a soirée tomorrow evening."

"Very good," she said, putting on a pretence of the very model of a dutiful wife. "I assume you require me to make the necessary arrangements. What sort of food shall I ask the cook to prepare?"

"There will be no need for food. Maybe some small aperitifs, but nothing more than that." A smile played on his lips, and she felt herself stiffen in response, knowing that he was deliberately toying with her, wanting her to ask.

She wanted so much to disappoint him, to stay mute and not satisfy his childish urges, but she knew that the fallout would be so much worse if she did so. She couldn't handle another one of his rages. And he would end up telling her anyway.

"Oh?" she asked, feigning curiosity. "What sort of party will this be?"

"Oh, not a party as such; more a séance."

She found herself gasping in spite of herself. "Why ever would we want to hold one of those… things?"

He chuckled. "I know such things do not chime with your *scientific* view of the world." He spat out the word as though it were a curse. "But there are plenty of people who are fully prepared to have open minds on the topic; and it is they who will be our guests."

"In that case, maybe I can be excused from this particular soirée? After all, I would not want to be the cause of any unhelpful auras or some such."

"Mind your tone!" he snapped, making her jump. "You will be there, as my dutiful wife. Is that understood? After all, Mr Emerson will be there, and he is ever so keen to see you again."

She felt a cold shiver run down her spine at the mention of that man. She had met Mr Emerson a handful of times, and each one had been distinctly unpleasant. Not because of anything in particular he had said or done, but more due to what was clearly not said. The man had a veneer of humanity which was only skin deep, while his eyes betrayed the terrors he was no doubt capable of.

Nevertheless, she swallowed, cast her eyes down, and gave her husband a brief nod.

"Good girl," he said under his breath.

There was a knock on the front door. After a moment, the living room door opened. "Mr Emerson here to see you, sir," said the butler.

"Ah good," said Marchant. "Send him through."

A moment later, a tall dark man entered the room, removing his black coat, which he handed to the butler along with his top hat. He wore an expensive black suit and carried a black cane topped with a silver topped ball which looked like a skull, gripped in a black gloved hand. He had a long, thin face which put Tessie in mind of a malnourished crow, topped with black hair which was groomed and waxed so much it almost shone.

But the most striking aspect of the man was his eyes. They were twin pools of blackness, sharp holes which seemed to suck in everything they regarded. Tessie felt herself shrinking away from their glare, hoping that he would ignore her and simply focus his attention on her husband.

Unfortunately that was not to be the case.

"My love," said Marchant. "You of course know my colleague, Mr Emerson."

She stood and forced herself to offer her hand to the man. "A pleasure, sir," she said.

He took her hand and raised it to his lips. She fought the urge to shrink away from their cold touch, gritting her teeth and forcing her mouth into a smile.

"Madam," he said, his voice low and slightly nasal. "The pleasure is all mine. Your husband speaks of you so much, I feel as though we are constant companions."

She looked up at Marchant. "Really?"

"Indeed," continued Emerson. "I understand you are quite a… singular young lady."

She felt her cheeks burn while her heart started to race.

Both men's eyes seemed to have a hungry look in them as they watched her. She had an overwhelming desire to be anywhere else, as quickly as possible, but Emerson had her hand in a tight grip.

"We were just talking about the event tomorrow evening," said Marchant. "Weren't we, dear?"

"Ah yes," said Emerson. "The séance. It should be such fun, do you not think?"

Tessie opened and closed her mouth, noticing how suddenly dry it was. Emerson's eyes seemed all-consuming, pulling on her focus like a magnet.

"We *so* agree," said Marchant, a leering grin on his face. "And we are so honoured that you will be joining us, Mr Emerson."

"You know I would not miss it for the world," he replied. "It should be a most… enlightening evening."

Tessie finally found her voice. Pulling her hand free from Emerson's, she cleared her throat and said, "If you will excuse me, gentlemen, I shall leave you to your business."

"But of course," said Emerson, stepping aside with a bow. "I look forward to spending more time with you tomorrow evening."

"And I," she said with a forced smile, nodding at them both and then turning and making her way to the door. It took an effort of will to not break into a run, all the time feeling their eyes on her back. As she closed the door, she heard Emerson say in a low voice, "She is perfect."

She shuddered and then ran up the stairs, throwing herself on her bed and burying her face in her pillows.

Chapter Eight

The past few days had been among the most stressful of Spencer's life, which was saying something. Stressful enough to make him seriously question his newfound choice of career. While the job for Mr Johnson had—to their great surprise—gone as planned, the demons had been quite upset to discover the dismembered remains of two of their number the next morning. Word quickly got out that there was a blood price on the heads of those who had killed the demons, and both Spencer and Bart knew that there was no shortage of people who would gladly shop them in, given half the chance: even to the demons.

Especially to the demons.

So they had spent the days since the job in a paranoid mess, constantly watching over their shoulders and keeping as far away from demon territory as they could. For once, they were glad of the constant police presence following them round, an inadvertent bodyguard on hand should anything happen.

It reminded him of his youth, of the endless days he'd spent on constant alert, running and hiding from one bully or another. And then, at the end of the day, there wasn't even safety to be found at home: every night his dad would come back from the pub, stinking of booze and looking for any opportunity to take out his frustrations on his family. Spencer, as the only son and a huge disappointment to his dad—too small, too scrawny—was, more often than not, the focus of the drunken rages. He'd tried keeping out of sight, but the cramped room they called home had precious little space to hide in. He had thought about running away, but he knew that would just mean his dad's fists would find another target. And the thought of his mum or sisters having to put up with that…

So Spencer had spent his childhood dodging fists, not only on the streets but at home as well. It had taught him some valuable skills: how to spot when the mood in a room was turning ugly, ways to avoid a fight. But he had hoped that when he grew up he'd not have to spend so much time running away. Hell, maybe he'd grow up to be big enough and strong enough to not be a target. Maybe he'd do the beating up instead.

Fat chance. He was still the victim, and had just swapped one lot of predators for another.

After a few days of not being killed by vengeful demons, he'd felt confident enough to start advertising for more work, and him and Bart ventured out onto the streets to stick up some more of their posters and spread the word.

The afternoon was drawing in as he fixed one of the last posters to a wall, not far from Covent Garden. As he was finishing up, Spencer felt a rough hand on his shoulder. "Well, well, well. If it ain't me old mate Spencer. I heard the police were all over you, that they'd banged you up."

Spencer turned slowly, arranging his face into as confident a smile as he could manage. "They couldn't make anything stick," he said.

Facing him were four smiling goons. The one who had had his hand on Spencer's shoulder peered past him then reached out, grabbed the poster, and ripped it off the wall. "What this then? You working for someone else now?" His voice was gently chiding but he glared menacingly at Spencer as he spoke.

Even though he had been expecting this, Spencer still found

himself struggling to keep his composure and to form the words. "No. No one else. Me and Bart are setting up on our own. We're going to try something different. Going straight, you see?"

The man stared at the paper, his lips moving slowly as he read the words. "Demon hunting?" He and his goons burst out laughing and Spencer fought the urge to react, to protest or, more likely, to join in and toady to them. Instead he forced his face into a very small smile; not so small as to be disrespectful but enough to show them that he acknowledged the joke. Not that he appreciated being the butt of it, of course. He glanced around. Where was Bart?

"That's actually quite a funny joke," the man said. "You two setting up on your own. That's very funny."

"It's not a joke," said Spencer, fighting the quiver in his voice. "We're not attached to any gangs right now, so we thought we'd do something different. Don't want to get banged up again, do we?"

The thug screwed the poster up into a ball and threw it on the ground. "Thing is, the likes of you don't get to set up your own business, not without checking with Milton first. Did you check with him first?"

Spencer glanced around and was rewarded with a slap across the side of his head. "Don't go looking for your trained monkey," the man snarled. "It's just us here. Well... did you ask permission?"

"I don't need no permission," blurted out Spencer. "I don't work for no one."

"But you're in Milton's manor. You know that everything that happens here needs to go through him first. Otherwise, how's he going to know when his cut is due to him?"

"I was just putting up a poster..."

"I thought you were smarter than this, Spencer," the man said, putting an arm around his shoulder. "The other one I could understand, but not you. You're smart enough to realise how these things work. You knew what you were doing, so why did you choose to disrespect the boss like this? Do you hate him that much?"

Spencer quickly shook his head. "No, of course not. I just thought… I was just putting up a poster…"

The thug grabbed Spencer's chin with the other hand. "Now, you see, everything in life has a price. You want to put something up in the boss's manor, you come to him and agree the price. That's only fair, right? And he'll take a slice of what you did the other night, too."

Spencer spluttered at the words without thinking. "But that's—"

The man's eyes narrowed to slits. "I really hope for the sake of your health that you weren't about to say 'unfair'," he said a low growl. "I really—"

A shadow fell over them. "Oi, Spencer, what's going on here?" asked Bart in a low growl.

The men turned to look up at Bart's huge, bulky, towering form. The lead thug swallowed, his composure slipping for a moment, and then he glanced at his fellows and took a deep breath. Squaring his shoulders he said, "Good. You're both here. You're coming with us."

"Where?" asked Bart.

"To see Milton. To straighten this whole thing out. He sent me for you anyways, but he'll be 'specially interested in this little side-line of yours." As Bart folded his arms, the man continued. "It's up to you how we do this. But sooner or later, you'll be facin' him. It'll look a sight better if you come of your own accord, rather than him having to go to a special effort to get you to him. Don't you think?"

Bart took a deep breath, but Spencer put a hand out to stop him. "He's right. Better to see what the big man wants now, than let it hang over us. We'll come without any fuss."

The men exhaled and a couple laughed quietly in relief. At a glare from their leader, they composed themselves and then started to lead Spencer and Bart through the streets.

Chapter Nine

The room was dark, the drawn curtains making it feel as though they had been transported to somewhere spectral and otherworldly. A tiny slit of daylight broke through on one side and motes of dust played in the light, like tiny faeries dancing for the pleasure of those watching. The guests all spoke in hushed tones, every one of them instinctively treating the eerie atmosphere with a deferential respect, not wanting to break the spell with jollity or raised voices. Conversation was stilted, punctuated by the rush of words and occasional stifled giggle of the terminally nervous. Occasionally someone would mention the word "Tappers" before glancing around while their friends frantically hushed them.

Tessie stood in the middle of the room, awkwardly trying to keep up a pretence of mingling, while at the same time trying to avoid any form of actual conversation. As she moved around, she had a distinct feeling of being on display, as though everyone was watching her, wanting to see what she did next. Even Margaret seemed to be keeping a discrete distance; whenever she tried to approach her, suddenly the other woman was either surrounded by others or nowhere to be seen. For want of something to do, Tessie exchanged a few brief words with one couple and then excused herself, only to find herself face to face with her husband's associate, Mr Emerson.

"Lady Marchant," he said, taking her hand and brushing it with his lips. She suppressed a shudder; his hand was again cold and felt almost slimy, like a fish. His eyes moved up to meet hers and she had to fight every urge to run away; those eyes were like twin pits of bottomless despair. "A pleasure to see you here."

"A pleasure to have you in our home, Mr Emerson." In spite of her best efforts, she could feel her voice shake. "Are you looking forward to the evening's entertainment?"

"Entertainment. What an interesting way to describe what is to come," he said coldly.

"Oh?" Her interest piqued and ire raised by the way he talked to her, she spoke before she could stop herself. "And what exactly is to come?"

He let out a low, rumbling laugh and took her hand again in his. "Power. More power than you could ever imagine."

She wanted more than anything to pull away her hand and turn and run, but she forced herself to remain stock still and fix her eyes on his. "For whom, exactly?"

"As always, my dear lady, that is the important question. For whom?"

A bell rang and they turned as one to face the doorway, where Marchant stood with the guest of honour at his side. Tessie gratefully took the opportunity to sidle away, losing herself in the crowd. She found herself a few paces away from the doorway and tried to slink away, trying not to look as though she were attempting to disassociate herself from something of which she did not approve.

"I would ask you all to be seated," said Marchant, guiding the guest of honour to the round table in the centre of the room. She was a slight, plump woman with pale and wrinkled skin peeking out from behind a heavy patterned veil. The tip of her veil covered her face, so that only a thin mouth was visible.

As one, the guests blinked and then moved awkwardly to the table, the thing which they had tried so hard to ignore since they first entered the room, the potential centre of power and ruin, dreams and nightmares.

Marchant cast a cold eye over each of them as they took their places, studiously avoiding his gaze. "I trust that you have all respected the directive to avoid any form of introductions." He turned and held out a hand to his wife. "My dear, do be seated."

Tessie glanced back at the door, hoping that someone would enter at the last minute and call her away. With such salvation denied her, she slowly walked over to the empty chair opposite her husband and sat down, avoiding the gazes of the others around her. She particularly kept her eyes away from Emerson, refusing to meet his cold gaze, and as a result missing the faint smile which played on his lips.

All eyes turned expectantly to the guest of honour, who had kept her eyes fixed on the table.

"You all know why we're here," said Marchant. "And you also know that you are expected to respect the privacy of our guest here, and stay silent unless you are addressed directly." He looked around the table. "Good." He nodded to the old woman next to him before asking, in a voice which was suddenly quiet and respectful: "Madame, when you are ready?"

She nodded briefly and everyone watched, braced for whatever would follow. They watched as she stayed motionless, holding their breaths and straining their ears for some sign of her powers; a muttered spell or the stirring of some spirit from the other side, maybe.

The grandfather clock in the corner ticked on, accentuating the silence as it stretched around them all. They glanced at each other, quick sideways glances which felt dangerous but also necessary, silently questioning their fellows, wondering if this was some elaborate joke which everyone else was playing on them. Or maybe this woman was a charlatan. Maybe—

"Everyone touch fingers with the people to either side of you," said the old woman in a shrill voice which broke the silence like a thunderclap. "Like so. All our hands should form an unbroken circle."

Hands were placed on the table and shuffled to either side to comply, neighbours smiling shyly at each other to apologise for the invasion of their privacy.

"Good," said the woman. "Then we begin." Her head and shoulders stiffened, and her mouth began to work soundlessly.

The air around the table began to thicken, so that it became hard to breathe and thoughts flitted away as though they were ships glimpsed through a thick fog, forms just about visible but then disappearing before they could be truly grasped. A chill descended on the room, a cold which penetrated to their very bones, freezing them in place. A mist started to swirl around them, and the participants glanced at it; could this be the Aether of which they had heard so much? Some said the Aether was dangerous, the stuff of nightmares, but others spoke of its wondrous powers, that it was the pathway to the spirit world and the secrets of life and death.

The misty fingers whipped around them, encircling and probing. Then the whisps gathered around the old woman before shooting straight out, across the table and at Tessie.

"Make sure the circle remains complete," barked the old woman. "Do not move your hands or the result could be fatal."

Everyone watched as the Aetheric mist enveloped Tessie, who in turn was shocked into immobility. She sat rigid as the sickly white tendrils embraced her, covering her head and body, leaving only her hands free, still touching the fingers of the neighbours who tried to shrink away on either side.

Then the spell broke and she let out a low moan which grew into a shriek so piercing that it was all that present could do to resist covering their ears.

Tessie threw herself backwards, breaking the circle of fingers. The furniture and ornaments rattled as the room seemed to suck in a deep breath, taking the mist with it. Everyone looked to the floor, at Tessie scrabbling backwards, wide-eyed panic on her face and hair sprawled haphazardly about her head. Her mouth opened and closed as she stared at her husband before throwing herself at the door, leaving the room in a stream of muffled sobs.

Marchant pursed his lips as he watched her go. "Well?" he asked.

"She is perfect," the old woman said.

Marchant looked over to Mr Emerson, who nodded curtly.

Chapter Ten

"Well, well, well," Milton's voice rang out as they made their way through the empty theatre towards the group of leering men gathered on the stage. "If it ain't me old friends, Spencer and Bart."

He was seated in the centre of the stage at the top of the room on a raised chair, looking like a would-be king surveying his subjects. His eyes were small black pebbles which glared from under thick eyebrows with a piercing malevolence. Both men approached nervously, pushed along by their guards.

Seth stood to the left of Milton, an evil smile playing on his lips, while on the other side squatted a young man with long brown hair, who was wearing an elegant suit and toying with the dust on the floor with the end of a cheap-looking cane. An actor of some sort, Spencer supposed from the look of him. A theatre was probably the right place for a person like that, although what Milton needed from an actor, he had no idea.

"Actually, lads, you're a bit early," continued Milton. "Although it'll be good for you to see this. Shuffle over to the side and make yourselves invisible, eh? I'll get round to you in a minute." He turned his head and gestured over to another group who were lingering at the far end of the room. "Bring him here."

Spencer and Bart, jostled over to the edge of the room,

watched as a large, burly man was practically carried over to the stage and dumped in front of the three men. He had started his progress through the room shouting and kicking against the men restraining him, but by the time he was placed in front of Milton he seemed to deflate, standing there shaking and quivering.

"I know him," said Bart. "That's Nicky Baxter."

"So it is," said Spencer. "Proper hard man. Makes a change to see him in this sort of state."

Nicky dropped to his knees. "Milton, I'm sorry. I told you I'd make it good, I really did. You know I'm good for it…"

Milton held up his hand and the other man immediately fell silent. "You've let me down, Nicky. I trusted you and you let me down."

"Please," he said. "I just need one more day. One day and I'll get it all for you. Double. I'll get you double."

Milton tutted. "Thing is, I've heard this from you way too many times now. And I've heard you've not only been letting me down, you've been mouthing off behind my back about how you don't need to pay me. Hurts my feelings, that does. Makes me wonder whether you respect me."

"Of course I do. I respect you, Milton. I—"

"You ever heard the phrase, '*Too little too late*?" asked Milton. "You see, that's where we are right now. But it's not just that: you've given me a problem. If I let you get away with this, then what does that say about me? I need to make an example of you."

"No. Please…!"

"Shh…" Milton leant forward, putting a finger to his lips. "I don't want to do this, but you've left me no choice. Have a bit of dignity. Face it like a man, eh?" He waved his other hand at the elegantly dressed young man stood to his right. "Thaddeus, he's all yours."

Thaddeus waited a moment, continuing to toy with his cane, almost as though he had not heard Milton's words. Then he slowly and deliberately drew himself up to his full height; at a good six feet tall, he towered over the others around him. He smoothed down his trousers and then walked round to the wing of the stage, descending the steps one by one, tap-tap-taping his cane as he did so. Nicky had gone slack-jawed with terror as he watched the man approach, no longer able to make any noise beyond a low keening.

Bart leaned in to Spencer. "Is it me, or don't he look more scared of that bloke than Milton?"

"Yeah," Spencer said softly. "Wonder why."

"You'll see soon enough," growled one of their guards. "Now, shut up and watch."

By now, Thaddeus was stood in front of an increasingly panicked Nicky, who had regained the ability to move his body and was starting to struggle against the guards holding him. The young man held his right hand in front of Nicky's face and slammed the cane on the ground, barking the word "Still!" at the same time as the sound of cane on ground cracked out. Instantly, Nicky froze, a glowing red halo surrounding him.

The guards stepped back, rather hastily, as Thaddeus paced round Nicky's inert body, chanting in a low voice. After he had completed two circuits around his victim, a haze seemed to emanate from the long-haired man, forming a web-like structure with Nicky at its centre. Nicky, himself, seemed to be quivering, as though struggling against invisible bindings.

A further two turns around Nicky and then Thaddeus stopped to stand in front of him. By now the hazy web was more like a fog, enveloping the still-immobile man, wrapping around him like an aethereal blanket. Nicky finally found the strength to make some noise—or maybe it was the other man's focus being split in too many ways for him to maintain fully whatever spell he had placed on him. Regardless, Nicky started to make noises: desperate, strangulated noises.

Spencer felt an overwhelming urge to run away. To run away and throw up. But, just like Nicky, he found that he couldn't move, instead fixated on the scene in front of them.

Thaddeus's chanting rose to a crescendo, his hand lifting in the air in time with the volume of his voice, and Nicky's body tensed and rose in tandem with these. Then he clenched his fist and, with a snarl, slammed it down to his side.

There was a moment of silence as the mist dissipated from around Nicky, leaving him standing there, swaying and blinking. Then he gasped and put a hand to his throat. His eyes looked as though they were about to burst from their sockets as his face went red, then a dark purple.

"He's choking," said Spencer. "Isn't anyone going to help him?"

Everyone in the room stood there and watched, spellbound by the sight. Nicky flailed with his arms, fell to his knees, and tried to shuffle forwards, reaching for the stage with his free hand, as though he were trying to beg the men leering down at him for some sort of release. Then he collapsed.

Spencer puffed out his cheeks. "That's quite a trick; making a man choke by magic," he muttered to Bart. "What's he do for starters, do you reckon? Make someone stub their toe by waving a wand at them?"

Bart shushed him and pointed. Spencer looked up to see Nicky's body jerking and shaking. Then the man's back arched and he drew in a wheezing breath, followed by an avalanche of coughing.

"Pick him up," said Milton. Two men rushed to obey, pulling Nicky up and holding his weak body between them.

"So, you can go," said Milton. "But you'll have to put up with the little punishment Thaddeus here has gifted you with. You see, from now until the end of your days, every hour you will suffer an agonising death, and then miraculously rise from the grave. Every. Single. Hour. Ain't that right, Thaddeus?"

Thaddeus nodded. "Just for a bit of variety," he said, "the curse is such that the manner of your death will vary each time. Maybe you'll choke, or burn, or suffer a thousand stabs. But either way it will be painful."

"Nice touch," said Milton.

Thaddeus nodded his head in a slight bow.

"Although I don't remember giving you that instruction," continued Milton. "I thought we'd agreed you'd follow my orders to the letter. Surely you know how important it is with these things that there are no unexpected surprises."

"Of course," Thaddeus said as he bowed his head once more. "We wouldn't want that. It won't happen again."

Spencer thought he caught an edge there, as though the long-haired magician was talking through gritted teeth.

"Throw him out," said Milton to the guards.

"Wait," said Nicky. "You can't leave me like this! If I bring you the money…"

"You're done," said Milton. "You'll be too busy dreading the next hour to worry about bringing me any money. You're going to do me a much better service, by showing everyone what happens if they try and cross me. Now get out."

Spencer flinched as Nicky's screams receded to the back of the room and then were cut off by the slamming of the door. Then he flinched again as Milton clapped his hands.

"Now, back to business," Milton said. "You two, come over here. Your turn."

Spencer put on his best smile as they were jostled forward. "Milton, me old mate…"

"I'm no mate of yours."

"'Course not. You're far too esteemed and important a… Look, whatever we've done…"

Milton leaned forward. "What do you *think* you've done?"

"I'm sure it's just a misunderstanding, whatever it is…"

Milton nodded to one of the men who had escorted them in, who in turn slammed a fist into Spencer's stomach, sending him falling to his knees in a coughing, moaning heap. Bart started towards him, but two knives appeared at his throat.

"Try it, sweetheart," growled one of the other men.

Bart glared at him as Milton stood up from his chair and walked slowly off the stage and down toward them. "You're a funny pair, you two. Never been the best earners. Not that threatening, or that smart. Plenty of times, back when we first started out, you ballsed up. But I let you work for me. I let you live. Funny thing that, eh?"

Spencer pulled himself to his feet. "It's because we was useful," he said, spitting on the floor.

Milton stared at him and then clapped his hands. "Exactly! You were useful, and you've kept on being useful. Getting rid of a competitor here or there, running the odd job which no one else would do. And besides, we were kids back then. Who didn't do stuff when they was kids, that they wouldn't do now?"

"I would," said Bart, fixing him with a stare and ignoring Spencer's pleading look. "Right now I'd do the same."

Milton returned the big man's stare. "Sometimes, Bart, I swear you actually do want to get killed. And yet still I let you live."

Spencer cut in before Bart could get himself into any more trouble. "Which makes me think we're still useful to you."

Milton stared at Bart for a moment longer and then snapped his head round to face Spencer. "As ever, you are correct." He turned and started to walk back up onto the stage. Spencer and Bart were ushered forward to follow; at a silent nod from Spencer, Bart reluctantly agreed to be escorted up.

"What is the most important thing to me?" Milton asked.

Spencer glanced around. "Money?"

Milton shook his head. "No. Money is important, but it's not the most important." He gestured around. "Surely you were paying attention to our little floor show just now?"

"Loyalty?" asked Bart, uncertainly.

Milton snapped his fingers. "Exactly. Loyalty. Without that, I could have all the money in the world, but it'd be worthless, could be taken away at any moment. I need loyalty." He turned around and stared at them. "You know where I'm going here, I take it."

The two men glanced at each other and then shrugged. "Not

really," said Spencer.

Milton tutted. "How do people show their loyalty to me?"

"Doing what you say?" asked Bart with a frown.

"No. Well, yes. But more than that. They show me respect by paying me tribute, paying me my cut, every time they do a job on my manor."

"Right…"

"And that's why I'm so unhappy with you two."

Spencer let out an exasperated chuckle. "Not sure if you noticed, but we tried to do some work for you, and your man Seth there told us to… what was the exact word, Bart?"

"Bugger off?"

Spencer clicked his fingers. "That's right. He told us to bugger off. We helped him on a job—a job for you—and he took away our cut."

Seth narrowed his eyes at them. "Do we have to go over that again? What you did to balls-up that job?"

"*Almost* balls-up the job," pointed out Spencer. "You still got your book thingummy."

"Wasn't really the most professional of jobs though, was it?"

"Well, look," Spencer squirmed. "You pay for results, right? We got you the result you wanted."

Milton held up a hand to stop them. "But then I hear that you've done another job."

"What?"

"You heard me. Up West. I hear you dealt with a couple of low-level demons for a shopkeeper."

"They weren't low-level," protested Bart. "They were bloody big things. Took a great big swing to get their heads off, it did."

Spencer winced as his friend spoke. "The thing is," he said slowly, gathering his thoughts. "Seth told us to…"

"I know what he told you," snapped Milton. "But what he didn't do was give you permission to go off and do stuff without my say-so."

"But we don't—"

"*But you do.*" Milton leaned in close. "This is my manor, and you are two small-time thieves who are only walking the streets because I allow you to. Without my protection you'd be banged up, or dead."

"Hah!" snorted Spencer, immediately regretting the outburst as all eyes in the room bore into him.

"Something funny?"

"I…" Spencer cast around for an excuse and then, with sinking resignation, simply decided to tell the truth. "I was just… It's just that we've got these bobbies crawling all over us, which made me think that your protection had been withdrawn."

Milton tutted. "How could I ever abandon you? But you see, here's the problem. You did a job in my manor, but you didn't ask for permission, and you didn't pay me no cut. That's not what loyal people do."

Spencer frowned. "We didn't pay you no cut because there was nothing to cut you in on. We made nothing from the job."

"DON'T LIE TO ME!" They all jumped as Milton bellowed at them. Then the big man cleared his throat and continued in a lower voice. "I'm not an idiot. I know exactly what you earned from him. And Bessie. And Mungo."

"Ah. Well." Spencer ran his fingers through his hair, then when they got stuck in the grimy tangle, slowly pulled them back out again. "You see…"

"It's all right," Milton smiled. "We're all grifters here. I'm sure we've all pocketed a bit from time to time. Kept a bit back for ourselves. That's the game, right?" He looked around the room.

Bart nodded and grinned, then stopped when Spencer elbowed him in the ribs. Everyone else was shaking their heads.

"You see, that's what loyalty looks like," said Milton. "That's what I expect." He leaned back in his chair and tapped his teeth with his fingers. "You see, today's your lucky day. I've already made an example of one idiot already. Be a bit wasteful to send another two broken souls out so soon, don't you think?"

"Absolutely." Spencer's mouth was suddenly very dry, and his heart was pounding. In his experience, bosses rarely dispensed good news, or let him get away with things.

"After all, you've seen what my pet magician here can do." Milton either didn't notice or care about the frosty look Thaddeus shot him at these words. "You can serve a purpose by spreading the word. Making sure everyone knows exactly what happened to Nicky, and why. Can't you?"

"Oh, yeah, with pleasure. I mean, we're great at spreading the word, ain't we, Bart?"

"I suppose…" Bart started. Then, noticing the glare from his friend, he frowned and after a moment's thought nodded. "Yeah. We definitely can do that. Great at that, we are."

"Good," said Milton. "It'll give you something to do while you're earning for me."

"Earning?" asked Spencer. "But I thought we were out?"

"Consider this your chance to redeem yourselves. You'll be kicking back to me on every job. And I expect a payment every week, regular as clockwork. At least ten bob. But I know you'll manage more than that."

"Ten…!"

"And for starters, you can give me my share of the three jobs you've done over the past week. Get it to me by midday tomorrow."

"But…!"

"And while I know you won't need any sort of incentive, I think I'll give you someone to watch over you, to keep you motivated and on the straight and narrow. Not that I don't trust you, you know, although I really, really don't." He gestured with his left hand. "Thaddeus here will keep an eye on you. And if you don't perform as required, I will allow him to practice some of his more… inventive curses on you."

This clearly came as a surprise to the magician, who turned and stared at Milton, but kept his silence.

"You're glocky," Spencer said. "You're proper mad. How are we ever going to get that sort of money that regular?"

"Don't know," shrugged Milton. "But I bet you're proper incentivised now, eh? Oh, and a little ground rule: your earnings have to be proper extras from what I'm already due, so no stealing from my turf. You earn from elsewhere, you hear? Now, leave."

Spencer shook his head as they turned to go.

"Oh, and another thing," said Milton from behind them. "You'll be wanting to be extra careful with your activities. Especially if the police are now paying attention to you. You don't want to get nicked; if you wind up in the clink, you'll lose the ability to earn, and… Well, you know what'll happen then, eh?" The laughter echoed around them as they left the theatre, thankfully cut off with the closing of the door behind them.

"What now?" Bart asked finally.

"In a word: we're buggered."

Chapter Eleven

Tessie took a deep breath as she took her seat, looking down over the rest of the theatre from the fine box Marchant had led her to. "You stay here," he ordered her before walking over to speak with the other men gathered at the rear of the box.

Tessie toyed with her theatre glasses, turning them around a few times before holding them up to her eyes to look around the finery of the Sadler's Wells theatre. The plays themselves usually bored her, which was just as well as her husband had no interest at all in the arts, only using their visits to the theatre as opportunities to hobnob, to see and be seen by the great and good. Forced once again into the role of quiet and dutiful wife, Tessie spent her time examining the architecture and ornamentation of the fine London theatres and, on occasion, enjoying the tricks the stage designers played to transform the simple stage space into somewhere exotic. For a brief period of time, she would allow herself to be transported by her imagination to a happier place: anywhere but where she was.

And then there were the people. She scanned the audience, busily finding their seats, chatting to old friends and new, sharing a joke or an intimate moment. A young couple towards the back were engaged in a whispered conversation, their faces flushed with the excitement of a new love. Her gaze lingered on the way the man gently stroked his lover's hand, the way she returned his affections with a smile and a lingering look. Tessie sighed. That should have been her. Instead…

"Another Shakespeare play. How ghastly." Lady Sinclair bustled into the seat next to her, arranging her skirts while flapping a programme at her. "Good afternoon, my dear. And how are you today?"

"I am fine, thank you." Tessie placed the eyeglasses back on her lap, that glimpsed perfect world now wrenched away from her. She had been told by Marchant that the Sinclairs would be joining them, and that she was to be as engaging and entertaining as she could. Something which was easily said than done; of all the people in London, Lady Sinclair was everything Tessie despised: a frightful, closed-minded snob with a love of gossip above everything. "How are you?" Tessie asked, fixing her face into a tight smile.

"Passable. I would be better if I didn't have to sit through this melodramatic twaddle, but there we go. All in the name of duty, eh?" She looked over her shoulder at the men then, satisfied that they were not listening in, leant in to Tessie and said softly, "But in all seriousness, how are you, dear? After that… event the other night?"

Tessie turned her head so that the other woman would not see her blushing. "I am fine," she muttered. "Just fine."

"But really," persisted Lady Sinclair. "That was quite the shock you gave us all, when you left the room so abruptly."

"I just had a funny turn." The line had been rehearsed so many times; anything to ensure she did not embarrass herself or her husband any further. "I needed a lie down. That is all."

"It looked like *more*," persisted Lady Sinclair. "There was talk around the table that you had been touched by some form of spirits. I do wonder: what does such a thing feel like?"

"I would not know." Tessie allowed a cold edge to slip into her voice. "Such things as spirits and séances are just so much nonsense: surely even you know that."

Lady Sinclair harrumphed. "I would not let your husband hear you said such a thing if I were you. He seemed very much taken by the medium and her skills. He and that delightful Mr Emerson were at pains to quiz her on so many aspects of her remarkable talents."

"Indeed." Tessie decided that a cold formality would be the best way to endure the next few hours; for once, she found herself willing the play to start, so there would be something to stop the woman's chatter.

"It could be," said Lady Sinclair, leaning in further, "that if you did display an aptitude for the supernatural, that would prove a fine way to keep your husband content with you. Heaven knows, you need something: it is certainly not your ability to entertain or keep house. Oh look: it appears the play is about to start."

Tessie held up the eyeglasses once more, pointing them in the vague direction of the stage but seeing nothing more than a blur as she tried in vain to blink away her tears.

*

At the interval, Tessie managed to get away from Lady Sinclair, using the sanctuary of a visit to the toilet to powder her nose as her excuse. On her way back, she was pleasantly surprised to see that Lady Sinclair had moved, and Margaret was now seated in her place.

Margaret watched her as she eased into her seat. "Tessie, it is so lovely to see you out and about once more," she said. "I take it you are now recovered from whatever ailment befell you at the séance?"

"Yes, thank you, Margaret," Tessie replied, arranging her skirts.

"I thought you could do with a change in theatre companion," Margaret said. "I am sorry that I did not have a chance to speak with you earlier, but your friend Lady Sinclair was monopolising your time, as usual."

Tessie gave a noncommittal "Hmm."

Margaret sighed. "I honestly do not know why you let that old hag push you around so much."

"She is a good woman," Tessie said dutifully. "She has my best interests at heart."

"You do not have to keep up that charade with me," Margaret said. "You know I would never confide in that old harridan."

Tessie quickly put a hand to her mouth to stifle a grin.

"That is better," smiled Margaret. "I do fear sometimes that you are being cowed far too much by that woman. Now, tell me: what is going on?"

She looked around, trying to convince herself that she was doing the right thing, whatever she decided to do. She could not shake the feeling that she was damned regardless: if she spoke her mind then she was betraying her husband and her family, but if she did not then surely she risked an even worse fate?

"I... am concerned," she said, forcing the words out. "Edward has been acting more and more bizarrely of late. I feel like I am his prisoner, rather than his wife. He entertains these strange people, taking them into his study and then refusing to talk to me about what is discussed."

"Have you asked him?"

"Of course."

"And?" prompted Margaret.

"At first he looked at me in a way which... It were almost as though he was sizing me up for something. It sounds silly, but that's the best way I can describe it; for a moment he looked at me like nothing more than a jewel or some other possession. But not in a good way. Like I was something to be sold, that he could make money from."

"You always complained that he did not seem to care enough about you," began Margaret.

"That is exactly what Lady Sinclair said. But that's not it; if you had seen the way he looked at me, the hunger in his eyes..."

She shuddered. "Then he snapped, and barked at me to mind my own business. Then there was that business at the séance the other night."

Margaret nodded slowly. "Yes. That was quite a performance, if I may say so." She studied Tessie's face. "You think these are all linked, that he is intending to do something to you."

Tessie nodded, wiping away a tear with the heel of her hand. "I am scared. I feel like I have become a prisoner in my own home, with no one to turn to, forced to wait until he does whatever it is he is planning. Which I fear will lead to no good for me." She looked up at Margaret. "You think I am being silly. That I am imaging all of this."

"Not at all," the other woman said. "Us girls need to stick together. It may be nothing more sinister than a mistress, or a failing business venture."

"I know he is disappointed that I have not become pregnant yet. Although he is hardly fulfilling his part in that department."

Margaret grinned. "That is better. A bit of fight, just like the Tessie I met when you first came down here. Let me see what I can find out. Maybe my Jonathan can shed some light on all of this."

Tessie started. "Please do not tell him what I said. If this gets back to Edward…"

"Do not worry. I will be the soul of discretion. You know how well I can handle my husband; the poor little dear will not know what he is telling me."

Chapter Twelve

"What's he doing?" Bart asked.

Spencer hissed at him to be quiet, then whispered, "He's still waiting. Freddie must be running late tonight."

"Why don't we just rob him while he's stood there all alone? We could give Milton all the loot."

"And he'll just make out that it's not even worth a fiver. Safer to actually have the coin in our hands. Trust me: I've been burnt like that too many times."

"I'm just not a fan of hanging round here, you know, just in case?" Bart looked around.

"In case what?" asked Spencer.

"You know, the *Tappers*?" Bart said the last bit as a whisper.

Spencer rolled his eyes. "I thought we'd agreed that was just some sort of fairy tale; something imagined up to scare folk. They're not real. And anyway, I've not heard any talk of them being around the docks."

"I knew it," Bart smiled triumphantly. "You're not sure if they're a story or not either, are you?"

"I dunno. But there's more important things to worry about. Like how if we don't do this job, we'll have Milton on our backs. Right?"

Bart shrugged and then turned to rest his back against the

wall. Spencer continued to watch their prey, a bent-backed man whose stance cleverly disguised a coat which, to the trained eye, was clearly bulging with loot. While the casual observer may have assumed from the way he held himself that he was an old man, they knew that he was in fact not much older than they were. The man they were watching was a nimble thief still very much in his prime. And he was currently in possession of a large quantity of jewels, with a buyer due to arrive at any moment. A buyer which Spencer and Bart fully intended to rob.

They had received the tip-off from an associate of theirs, someone who owed them a favour and had been persuaded—through the medium of Bart's fists—to repay them through information. Although, as they waited there, Spencer wondered if this wasn't some sort of set-up, another way for Milton to torment them even further.

And so they found themselves at Victoria Docks, huddled round the back of a pile of crates, waiting for Freddie the fence to meet the thief they were currently stalking. The docks were winding up for the evening, the last ships mostly unloaded and the sailors having decanted off to the nearest pubs and brothels. Seagulls whirled and shrieked overhead, desperately searching for scraps and waste, emboldened by the fact that the humans below had thinned out. All pervading was the stench of fish, which almost, but not quite, masked the foulness of the Thames.

Spencer was broken from his thoughts by Bart, tapping him—hard—on the back and half-bellowing, "Bugger me, what's that?"

Spencer jumped and pressed himself back against the wall, biting back a stream of curses. "You know these jobs work best when the bloke we're sneakin' up on doesn't know we're here, right?"

"Yeah, but what the hell is that? It's not another one of them demons, is it? I thought we'd given them the slip." Bart pointed at a massive shadow which was lumbering towards them, a mountain which walked on two legs as it stepped over crates as though they were a child's toys. It was roughly shaped like a man, albeit one made purely out of clay. Each arm was the size and length of a good-sized horse, while its body was a rounded mass which would have rivalled the finest carriage in bulk. On top of all this squatted a rounded head, the only features on which were two small eyes which glowed a bright red like twin coals.

"Nah, that's not a demon," said Spencer as the creature paused ten feet or so away, staring at them impassively. "You remember them golems which messed up the East End a while back?"

"Is that what they looked like?" Bart asked. "I heard one was made tame."

"That's right. Folk say they don't really have thoughts of their own: there's some words you put in their heads that control them. I think the words in this one's head tell it to fetch and carry and the like." He clicked his fingers. "Actually, I heard it was told to obey and protect humans. Useful, eh?"

"Clever," muttered Bart. "What's it doing here?"

"Last I'd heard, once it ran out of demons to fight it decided to make itself useful fetching and carrying down here at Vicky Docks."

Bart stared at the creature, which seemed to be staring impassively back at them. "Looks like it's having a break from work, hey?"

"Do you two always talk this much?" asked Thaddeus from behind them. "I thought this was supposed to be a stealth job."

"You've got a point," said Spencer. "But you've seen how hard it is to get this one to keep shtum. Anyway, it's loud enough round here with all the other noise for that bloke to not hear us. And let's face it, sitting round being silent gets real boring, don't you think?"

"After sitting here listening to you two prattle on," said the magician, "I would welcome some boring silence." He glared at them. "Maybe that could be arranged…"

"Now hold on," said Spencer. "Pretty sure Milton didn't give you permission to do that. After all, how can we earn if we can't talk?"

"Permission?" spat Thaddeus. "I do not need permission from that—"

They heard muttering from behind them and switched their attention back to the scene around the corner. They had clearly missed the bulk of the transaction, as both men were in the process of swapping bundles, glancing furtively around.

The thief, who had previously been hunched over, had relieved himself of his wares and as a result now quite literally seemed to be a different man. He stood around six foot tall, and where before he had given the impression of being an old man, was now revealed to be in his late teens at most.

Freddie, on the other hand, was as recognisable as ever: a short, stocky ginger man flanked by two huge bodyguards.

Spencer put a hand on Bart's arm. "Get ready," he muttered. "As soon as that tall bloke passes us, we pounce. Got it?"

The tall thief started walking straight back towards them. Spencer and Bart squeezed themselves back around the corner, knives drawn.

As he passed them, both men stepped out and matched his pace, walking either side of him. The thief glanced at them and then turned to dart away, only to be pulled short by Bart's firm hand on his shoulder. Thrown to the ground, he struggled to pull a knife from his pocket, but it was kicked out of his hand by Spencer.

"Evenin' mate," said Spencer. "How about we do this the easy way, and no one gets hurt, eh?"

Before the thief could answer, a bellow made them all turn to look back to see Freddie and his guards charging towards them. They stopped a few feet away.

Freddie glared at them. "Do you really think I'd let you steal from a client so soon after they've dealt with me? You realise the damage that sort of thing can do to business?"

"What, you're the only one allowed to steal from people

round here, that it?" sneered Spencer.

"Oi! What do you mean?" the thief asked, still sprawled on the ground. "I got a fair price."

"Yeah, you keep telling yourself that, sweetheart," said Spencer. "Looks like we got ourselves a bit of a—"

"There they are!" They all turned at the sound of a mighty bellow from behind them to see two demons lumbering towards them. "That's the two we've been after."

Spencer muttered a collection of choice swear words.

"Thought you said we'd given them the slip," said Bart.

"Yes, well I thought we had," said Spencer. "Clearly I was being optimistic." Inspiration struck him, and he looked down at the thief. "I'd give us your money now, mate."

"What?" the man said, transfixed by the demons bearing down on them.

"Your money. Give us it all now, or we'll get our pet demons there to tear you to pieces."

"'Ere," started Freddie. "You can't do that. My boys'll—"

"What boys?" asked Bart.

Freddie glanced round to see that his comrades had bolted. Then he saw the demons getting closer and closer, and what was left of his nerves disappeared. He turned and ran.

The thief turned out his pockets, handing the contents to Spencer with shaking hands.

Spencer's mouth worked as he counted the coins. "You were done, mate," he muttered as the man turned and ran away as well.

"What now?" asked Bart. "We run too?"

Spencer licked his lips, glancing over to the side. "In one moment."

"But…"

"Mate, if we run now, we'll just be two idiots running away from two big demons. I've got an idea."

"Better be a good one. In case you ain't noticed, they're getting pretty close. And I left me axe at home. Why did I leave me axe at home?"

"If I'm right, we won't need any axes," said Spencer.

"If you're expecting me to do anything, you're sadly mistaken," said Thaddeus. "I'm only here to make sure you give Milton his share. I won't be getting in the way of any fight you have with the demons. But I will make sure I rescue the money from your corpses; unless you'd rather give it to me now, save me waiting?"

Spencer shot him a glare. "No thank you. We'll deliver it ourselves when we're done with this."

Thaddeus shrugged. "Suit yourself. I'm going to stand a little way back. Don't want to get blood on my suit, you understand."

"Of course."

"When they start tearing you to pieces, if you could maybe throw the purse in this direction, that would be appreciated. Save me having to wade through your entrails."

"Why don't you help us?" asked Bart. "We're worth more to Milton alive than dead."

"Barely," said Thaddeus. "And his *instructions*," he spat the word out, "didn't extend to putting myself in harm's way or using any of my powers against demons. I am certainly not going to risk my neck for you two, or for him. And anyway, I won't get involved in something like this. I won't use my powers in that way. I have morals."

"Morals!" laughed Spencer. "We literally saw you curse a man to never-ending painful deaths!"

The demons were still making their noisy way towards them, only a handful of yards away by now, although they had slowed slightly, cocking their heads as they regarded the two men.

"They don't know why we're not running," said Bart. "This your plan? Confuse them to death?"

"Not quite," said Spencer, looking round. "I've got a theory; although I'm now starting to wonder whether it's actually a good one." He grabbed Bart's arm. "Get ready to run, all right?"

"Yeah," Bart said, wide-eyed, as the demons reared above them, ready to strike.

Then the crate nearest to them exploded inwards, followed by a huge clay fist which pummelled into the nearest demon, sending it flying into its comrade, both of them sprawling to the ground. The golem emerged and threw itself at the demons, fists and feet beating into the creatures, not giving them a moment to recover.

"Now!" barked Spencer. "Run!"

They both turned and sprinted away, weaving through crates and then streets, putting as much distance between themselves and the demons as they possibly could. Finally, when they could run no further, they collapsed behind a wall, gasping for breath.

A few moments later, Thaddeus sauntered round. "Clever," he said. "You knew the golem would protect you from the demons."

"Yeah," panted Spencer. "Or at least I hoped so. I remembered someone telling me the words in that thing's head—"

"The *Shem*," said Thaddeus.

"Bless you."

"No," Thaddeus rolled his eyes. "That's what it's called: the instructions in the golem's head which animate it and direct its actions. It's called the golem's *Shem*."

"Great. Yeah. Well, I heard it basically ordered it to protect the humans."

"Bit of a gamble to assume the golem would assume the instructions extended to you, don't you think?" asked Thaddeus. "And what if someone had changed the instructions since whenever you'd been told that story?"

Spencer shrugged. "Well, you know, not sure if you noticed but we were in a bit of a tight spot. Not too many options. Sometimes you need to take risks, savvy?"

"Indeed," said Thaddeus. "Anyway, this has been an entertaining diversion; I'll be taking Milton's share of what you earned. And a bit more for myself."

"What?"

"Call it a little way of thanking me for not cursing you."

"But you did nothing! You could've helped us then and you—"

"I didn't kill you," Thaddeus observed. "I could have ended it for you a lot sooner. Be thankful I allowed you to continue with your foolhardy plan. And that I continue to allow you to live, without pain."

Spencer glared at him and then pulled out the purse, counting out the coins. He passed a pile to Thaddeus, who continued to hold his hand out. Muttering a few more swear words, Spencer added more coins until the magician nodded, satisfied.

"Been a pleasure doing business with you, gentlemen. I will catch up with you at some point in the next few days, when you are next doing something profitable. And don't worry; I will know where you are." With that, he turned and walked away, tapping his cane on the ground in a hauntingly merry tune as he did so.

Spencer looked down at what was left in his hand.

"What we got?" asked Bart.

"Enough for a couple beers; that's about it," said Spencer. "Suppose we should be grateful them bobbies weren't sniffing around as well, eh? Come on: let's get drunk and think about how we're next going to earn. Ideally without risking a pummelling from them demons."

*

"Margaret!" Tessie waved as she hastened across the street after her friend, who showed no sign of having noticed her. "Margaret!"

One of the ladies with Margaret looked over her shoulder and then said something, gesturing back. Margaret shook her head and quickened her pace.

"Margaret, please, can I have a word?" Tessie was making a scene now and she knew it, but she was too far gone to do anything other than press on.

With a slump of her shoulders, Margaret gestured to her

companions to keep walking and then turned, a fixed smile on her face.

"Tessie, what are you doing? The entire street is looking at you!"

"I needed to talk to you; it has been a couple of days and I was wondering if you had found out anything about… you know…"

"The delicate matter you wished to keep secret? And you do that by bellowing in the street like a common market trader?"

Tessie opened her mouth in shock, her cheeks reddening. "I have been beside myself with worry. I just need to know."

Margaret glanced around, then back at her companions who were waiting, just out of earshot, whispering to each other as they watched the exchange.

"I should not be seen with you," she hissed. "The best thing that you can do is to go back to your home, keep your mouth closed and do as your husband bids you to."

"But…"

"No. This has gone on long enough. You have an overactive imagination, that is all. You behaved like a hysterical child at the séance and would have us all dragged into your pathetic little fantasies. I would ask that you leave me alone."

Tessie stared at her. "You said…" Her eyes opened wider as she started to understand. "Your husband; what did he say to you?"

"Nothing for you to worry about. You should concern yourself more with your own affairs. You have a good life, a good husband. If you persist in rocking the boat, then you will lose all of that. If that is what you want, then so be it, but I will not have myself dragged down with you." She turned and marched off.

Tessie watched her go, tears pricking at her eyes and a hard lump in her throat. She felt as though she had been slapped across the face.

Suddenly aware of the eyes on her, she recovered her bearing and strode back toward her house, her mind spinning as she fought to keep her breath steady.

Chapter Thirteen

Tessie stood outside Mr Johnson's coffee shop, fighting to calm herself down, her mind reeling with the thought of how completely and utterly alone she felt.

After her run-in with Margaret she had paced the streets, oblivious to everyone and everything around her. All she could think of was that her life was falling to pieces around her, with no one left that she could rely on, and a husband who seemed determined to... Do what?

She kept reliving, over and over, the events of the séance, dwelling on what had happened and how he had reacted. The hungry look in Mr Emerson's cold, black eyes. Those two men clearly did not have her best interests at heart, that was something she had suspected for some time. But Margaret's reaction had showed her that she now had no one she could trust. She thought back to all of the people at the séance: the great and good of London society. There had been some incredibly powerful people there. If they were all tied up in whatever dastardly scheme her husband was plotting, then she truly had nowhere to turn.

So she couldn't trust anyone she knew, or anyone who mingled in the same society as her or her husband. In a flash she had had her answer—her only option—and that was how she ended up at Mr Johnson's coffee shop.

She remembered the two odd gentlemen she had seen there, and the strange pamphlets they had been handing out. Demon hunting: that had been the gist of it. She knew that, by seeking them out, she was clutching at straws, but she had precious few other options.

She walked in and looked around, checking that there was no one in there she recognised. Thankfully it was fairly quiet at that time of day.

Mr Johnson bustled over to her. "Lady Marchant, a pleasure to see you here. A table for just yourself, or are you expecting company?"

"Just… Just myself, please," she said, her voice cracking as she tried to speak. "In the far corner, perhaps." She indicated a table furthest from sight from the street; she did not want to risk being seen. She allowed him to lead her over to the table and ordered a pot of tea.

As she waited she took deep breaths, working up the courage to do what was needed. She looked around in the hope that she would see the two odd gentlemen, although she was not sure what she would do if she did see them: from memory they were both terrifying-looking.

She nearly jumped out of her skin when Mr Johnson appeared at her table with her drink. Calming herself down as he served her, she took one more breath as he stood back.

"Would you like anything else, Lady Marchant?" he asked.

She cleared her throat. "Actually, yes. I noticed a couple of rather… unusual gentlemen here the other day. Rather rough-looking fellows, who you were talking with when my husband and I entered?"

Mr Johnson frowned and then shook his head. "I am not sure who you are referring to. We have a lot of different customers here; I am sure you understand." However, Tessie noticed the way he had stiffened and glanced around them, the way his cheeks reddened. "Now if that is all…"

"No," said Tessie, suddenly emboldened by the man's

94

discomfort. "If I were of a mind to speak to those fellows, would you be able to contact them on my behalf?"

"I told you," stammered Mr Johnson, "I do not know who you are speaking of." He glanced up and over her shoulder quickly.

Tessie turned to follow his gaze and noticed that the doorway leading to the rear of the shop was covered over with cloth, barely hiding some damage done to the door and frame. She had been prepared to beg Mr Johnson to keep her inquiries a secret, to make sure that her husband and his friends would not find out about her interest; but now she realised that actually the shopkeeper had more to lose by the truth being out than she did.

She turned back to face him, newfound confidence coursing through her as she smiled at him. "Whatever business you have with them is your business. I have no interest in that. You can rely on my total discretion, and I am sure I can rely on yours." She stared at him until he nodded hastily and then continued. "I would simply like a message to be given to them. You would know where to find them to deliver this message?" Another hasty nod. "Excellent. Then please tell them that they should meet a maidservant named… Molly, tomorrow in Hyde Park at five in the evening. By the bandstand on the north bank of the Serpentine. Can you do me this small favour?"

He nodded again.

"Excellent," she grinned. "Then I shall enjoy my tea while you deliver my message."

*

If he was being truly honest with himself, there were precious few things that Spencer was anywhere near an expert at. But reading people, cutting through the front that they showed the world, to reveal the truth of who they were: that was definitely one thing he was very, very good at.

When it came to this so-called maidservant, there was

something definitely off. She was too nervous for starters; much more than you'd expect, if she was just afraid of being caught by her employers. She jumped at the slightest movement, as though worried that the shadows would attack her at any moment.

Then there was the accent. Spencer knew that many of the well-to-do families would often send their children into service—either through necessity or to build relationships with a family higher up the social scale to them—but this maidservant's accent was far too refined for a common-or-garden servant. Usually, no matter where they were from, a bit of rough rubbed off on them in short order, even if it was just a dropped letter here or there, or a common phrase. But this woman had none of that; she'd clearly only ever spoken with them below stairs to issue orders.

But the clincher was the way she was acting. Centuries of in-breeding and entitlement had given the toffs a particular way of being, of acting and walking and talking, which no amount of play-acting could hide: especially not someone who clearly wasn't used to trying to pull the wool over peoples' eyes.

There was no doubting that this so-called maidservant was anything but, although she seemed determined to put on a front of pretending to be something she wasn't. Spencer decided to play along for the time being, to try and find out why she was trying to hide what she was. If nothing else, it gave him a power over her, and it wasn't often he had that sort of luxury.

"My mistress is concerned about the actions of her husband," she said. "She wishes to know if he is being faithful to her. She wants you to follow him around and report back to me as to whom he meets with and what he does."

"Sounds like a lot of work," sniffed Spencer. "Not really the sort of thing we'd normally do."

"She is willing to pay handsomely for your services," she said.

Spencer looked at Bart, who had been nodding along with her words, a distant grin on his face as he stared at her. He was clearly going to be worse than useless in any negotiation.

"How handsomely?" Spencer asked the girl.

She blinked at him. "Shall we say ten pounds per day?"

"Each," said Spencer.

"Agreed," she said, with barely a hesitation, and it was this which decided it for Spencer. Only a toff with no experience of household accounts would have agreed to such a ridiculous amount. Unless, of course, she really was desperate.

"I'm curious, though," said Spencer. "Why us?"

"You have been advertising your services."

"Yeah, as demon hunters. Not for spying on cheatin' husbands."

Was that a flinch which passed across her face? "Your visit was timely, as my mistress had been looking for people with your obvious talents."

Trying to con us with flattery, eh? Spencer thought. *Like that'll work!* Then he glanced over at his friend, who was lapping it up like a cat in front of the world's biggest bowl of cream.

"Of course," she said, a touch of steel in her voice now, "if this assignment is beyond you, or you do not wish to take my money, then I can of course go and find someone else."

Spencer held up his hands but, before he could say anything, Bart spluttered, "No, no, that's fine: we'll do it."

Spencer frowned at him, then, trying to regain the initiative, said, "We'll want paying up front. Two days' wages."

"One," she said. "I have twenty pounds here." She reached into her skirts and held out a purse. "Take it or leave it."

No sooner had the money been produced than it disappeared into Spencer's coat. "All right," he said, trying to sound as business-like as he could. "If we're going to do this, we need a few details. First, your name. Need to know who we're dealin' with."

"I'm… My name is… Molly."

"All right, Molly, nice to make your acquaintance, but we knew that. What's the name of your mistress and her husband?"

She started to speak, but then pulled herself up. "I would rather not give you names. All of your dealings will be through me."

Spencer scratched his head. "Yeah. You see, the problem is, it's going to be mighty difficult to follow round and report on someone if we don't actually know who they are. You follow?"

She frowned and then blushed. "I suppose… Although I need to know that you will respect the confidentiality of our arrangement…"

Spencer held up his hands in mock shock. "We are professionals, madame. We would never abuse our relationship by spreading gossip. As long as you keep your end of the bargain and pay us, we'll keep our end."

She seemed to be fighting a battle inside her head. "I suppose if I just gave you his name, but no… you would be able to…" She took a deep breath and then nodded, as though she had just decided to plunge into an icy pool. "His name is Lord Edward Marchant. He lives on Jermyn Street." She looked at them with wide eyes.

"Great," grinned Spencer. "And I take it our client is Lady Marchant."

She nodded quickly, glancing around with darting eyes.

"We need to know what he looks like and where to find him, to start us off, like. Do you know where he should be, this time of day?"

"Yes. He should be at his office, on Threadneedle Street. Do you know it?"

"Better if you take us there," said Spencer. "That way, you can point him out to us."

She shook her head rapidly. "Oh no, I could not possibly… What if he saw me?"

"Don't worry," said Bart. "We'll keep you out of sight."

*

As they walked along the street, Spencer and Bart held a huddled conversation just out of the maidservant's earshot.

"We can't do it," said Bart.

Spencer threw his hands in the air. "What do you mean, we can't do it? You heard her; you saw how much money she's willing to pay us. Think of how much pie and booze we can buy with that! Plus it'll keep Milton's pet magician out of our hair for a bit, if he makes an appearance again."

"Yeah. But we can't do it, can we?"

"Why not?" asked Spencer, putting his hands on his hips.

"But I thought we were supposed to be going straight, doing something legit for a change?"

"And we are," pointed out Spencer. "That's exactly what we're doing. We are offering a legitimate service to a young noblewoman. That's the beauty of it: the bobbies can follow us all they want, but they can't touch us for it."

"But I thought we were supposed to be huntin' demons?" asked Bart, trying a different tack.

"You said yourself just yesterday that we're not the best at that," pointed out Spencer. "You should be happy that we're taking on somethin' a bit more in our sphere of expertise. Plans change all the time; the trick is to make sure you move with them. That's the way to make a real success of things."

"Yeah, but…" Bart looked back at the woman. "But we were supposed to be going legit," he said again.

"And we are. We're helpin' her out with a problem."

"But she wants us to spy on her boss. Ain't there laws against that sort of thing? What if we find somethin'? Her mistress won't be happy."

Spencer frowned at his friend. "Since when has the happiness of some random toff got anythin' to do with it?"

"I dunno," Bart kicked at the grass. "I always find that the knowin' is sometimes worse than the not knowin'. Maybe she's better off not knowin' and just getting on with her life."

Spencer put an arm round his friend's shoulders, having to stretch to reach up, even though Bart was slightly slumped over as he walked. "Mate. If we go over to her and say that, what you think's goin' to happen? She'll go straight on to someone else who will take her money. And maybe that person ain't as trustworthy as us. She's got an itch, and you know what folks is like if they have an itch: gotta scratch it."

"I don't know…"

Spencer reached up to put a hand on his friend's shoulder. "Look. Just trust me. When have I ever let you down?"

"Well…"

Spencer grinned, clapping Bart on the shoulder before turning to walk back to the maidservant before he could answer. "Good lad! I knew you'd see sense."

*

Half an hour later, they were trying to lose themselves in the bustle of Threadneedle Street, watching bankers, businessmen and the generally well-to-do as they filled the pavements, making their way to some important meeting or another. Spencer, Bart and 'Molly' huddled across the road from Lord Marchant's offices, the two men taking care to keep themselves between the maidservant and any prying eyes.

"So how long you worked for these Marchant characters, then?" Spencer asked her.

"Oh, a few years."

"D'you like it? Working for them?"

"Oh yes. They're very kind to me. Especially Lady Marchant."

"I bet." He shared a glance with Bart, but the larger man was totally oblivious to his suspicions.

"So what sort of maidservantin' do you do then?"

"I work for Lady Marchant. I do whatever is asked of me: dressing her, helping with errands, and so on." She peered round Bart's body at a figure which had emerged on the far side of the street. "That is him, the one in the tall hat."

Spencer followed where she had indicated. There were a dozen men or more who were wearing tall hats. "You're going to have to narrow it down a bit, love."

"There, just walking past the haberdashers' shop. He has a brown cane in his hand and has a black beard. You see?"

"Got him." Spencer frowned as he stared at the man. He had that same walk that all toffs had, like he owned the street and everything around him. Probably never done a day's work in his life, just lived off the sweat of others. Spencer took a few moments to make sure he'd properly memorised the man: his face, the dark hair, trimmed beard, the way he glanced around all the time. "Yep, he looks suspicious, all right. You did well to get us involved in this. We'll get this sorted in no time."

"You will?" the girl looked at him with pleading eyes.

"Of course. Easy as pie."

"Tessie? Tessie Marchant, is that you?" A woman was walking towards them.

"We should be off," said the maidservant quickly, turning her head the other way. "I will show you where else he is likely to be."

"Tessie?" the woman said again.

"I think she's talkin' to you," said Bart. "But she doesn't seem to know what your name is."

"Let's go," said the maidservant.

"Tessie, it is you! What on Earth are you doing dressed like that?" The other woman was hurrying across the road towards them.

The maidservant glanced round, her eyes wide and cheeks pale. Then she turned and ran.

The woman stared after her, and then turned to Spencer and Bart. "What were you doing with my friend? And why was she dressed like that?"

"Don't know what you mean, love," said Spencer. "That's an old friend of ours."

"Then why did she run away?"

"She gets scared easily. 'Specially by toffs shouting strange names at her. Come on, Bart, let's get after her."

They sprinted off in the direction the girl had gone, but she had already lost herself in the crowds.

Spencer muttered a collection of swear words as he spun round. "Can you see anything?"

"Nope," said Bart. "But she's probably just gone back to her home, ain't she? Maybe she was late for work or something?"

Spencer shook his head. "We've got to find her before something happens to her."

Bart frowned. "Why are you so worried about her all of a sudden?"

"Because if something happens to her, we don't get paid!"

"But we'd just go to her boss, that Lady Marchant bird."

"Lady Tessie Marchant, you mean?"

"Yeah, I guess." Bart frowned in sudden realisation. "Here, that's what that woman was callin' after her just now. Funny that she looks just like her boss, ain't it?"

"It would be," prompted Spencer. "Unless…?"

"Yeah." A pause. "Oh." Bart's jaw dropped. "You mean…?"

"Yes."

"She was really…?"

"Yes."

"And she's gone runnin' off into the East End on her own."

"Yes."

"Oh. That's a bit dangerous for a toff lady, ain't it?"

"Just a bit," Spencer pointed to a fork in the road. "You take that side, I'll go down the other. We need to find her before someone else does, or we're not getting paid."

"What you mean? She'll hire someone else?"

"No," Spencer said patiently. "I mean it'd be pretty hard for her to carry on paying us if she's been stabbed to death."

Chapter Fourteen

Tessie ran through crowds of blurred faces, her heart beating an overly-loud tattoo, taunting her and making everything seem strange and other-worldly. She bounced from one body to another, her haste making her clumsy. A mass of faces snarled and leered at her, swimming round and around her.

The buildings loomed over her more and more, ramshackle dwellings reaching over the muddy street to each other, like bent-backed old men trying to shake hands across a chasm. Her feet splashed in puddles full of stuff that she dared not think of. The more she ran the poorer the condition of the houses, walls caked in mud and soot and effluent. And the smell…

How could she have been so stupid? She had been recognised, and now everyone would be talking about not only her strange reaction to the séance but now her wandering the streets dressed as a common servant. They had all been right: she should have kept her peace, remembered her place, not done anything to rock the boat. Now her husband would know all about her suspicions, and would no doubt make her suffer for them.

She ran to the side of the street and pressed herself back against the wall, fighting to catch her breath. She looked around, suddenly realising that she had no idea where she was.

The street she was stood on was grimy and overcrowded, full

of the sounds of hundreds of people all competing to be heard over each other. Costermongers bellowed their wares whilst children ran around shouting and screaming, accompanied by the loud curses of the adults they tripped up and—in a number of cases—pickpocketed.

The noise was bad, but the smell was overwhelming: a pungent mixture of body odour, foods and meats in various states of decay, and faecal matter. Indeed, the street itself was more like an open sewer, fed by buckets slopped down from the windows above as well as the litter and spoil from the animals and people who occupied what passed for a road and pavement.

She became aware of a number of people watching her with hungry looks on their faces. Feeling self-conscious, and her heart pounding that little bit faster, she turned and started to walk back in what she thought was the direction she had come from. She wrapped her arms around herself, suddenly aware of how much finer even her borrowed uniform was compared to those around her, and very conscious of how alone she was in that street full of strangers.

The nape of her neck itched with a feeling that she was being watched. She chanced a glance backwards to see a pair of ugly, dirty brutes staring at her intently as they stomped in her wake.

Her heart pounded harder as she turned back and started walking faster, stumbling over the uneven surface as she did so. She could hear their footsteps behind her, almost feel their putrid breaths on her back, imagined them grabbing at her arms and pulling her back, forcing all manner of unspeakable things upon her.

She came to a left-hand turning and, without thinking, immediately took it, darting down in the hope of slipping away from her pursuers. With a sinking heart she realised that it was practically deserted, the crowds replaced with a sparse stillness which left her with no hiding places.

She turned back, hoping to run back into the now-comforting busyness of the street, only to be faced with the leering grins of her pursuers.

She decided to chance a look of indifference and put her head down, marching past them in the hope that they were simply going the same way as her, rather than trying to trap her.

One of the men moved to block her way.

"Excuse me," Tessie said quietly.

"Going somewhere, Miss?" the man asked with a toothy snarl.

"Please, let me get past," Tessie said, stepping to the side and feeling tears prick at her eyes as the man moved with her to remain in her way. In that moment she was a young girl again, being teased by the others for not fitting in, not playing the way they wanted her to play. She could hear the laughter and taunts coming back to her over the years, making her want to curl up into a tight ball until it all went away.

Except that this time she was not faced with children, but with grown men. She was grabbed from behind, rough hands pinning her arms to her side. She let out a scream, which was cut short by the man in front of her stepping close and pressing his hand over her mouth. She pressed her lips tight, to try and avoid the pungent smell and taste of the man's fingers, but could not help but gag: it seemed as though the man had never been near a basin of water or a bar of soap in his life.

The man leaned over her and leered with jagged, stained teeth, his breath making her eyes water. "No point making a fuss, Miss, there's no one round here who'll stop to help you. We'll do you a deal: you make this easy, and we'll try our best not to hurt you. You never know, you might even enjoy it."

She struggled against them, but they were too strong, fingers already tearing at her clothes and pulling her skirt up to expose her legs. She brought her right knee up as hard as she could and allowed herself a brief moment of satisfaction as the man in front of her staggered back with a yelp. Any joy she felt was short-lived, though, as the man lurched back toward her, an angry snarl on his face.

"Oi, you," a voice bellowed from behind them. "Get off her now!"

Tessie found herself thrown to the ground as her attackers were forced to deal with this new threat, the wind pummelled from her lungs by the sudden impact with the ground. She looked up, swallowing back the metallic taste of blood in her mouth as she tried to make sense of the scuffling bodies in front of her.

One of her attackers flew through the air towards her, and she scrambled back and to the side before he could land on her, letting out a gasp as his bloodied face bounced off the stony ground. She backed away, scrabbling on hands and knees, unable to tear her eyes from the unconscious figure. Then a huge, slab-like hand appeared in front of her. She looked up to see the large, bald man: Bart.

"You all right love—erm, Miss—erm milady?"

She nodded, accepting his hand and allowing herself to be pulled to her feet.

"Yes, thank you. You saved me… thank you."

They looked up at the sound of footsteps from the entrance of the street. Half a dozen men were walking towards them, clearly upset at the sight of the two men lying bloodied on the floor. One of the men held a club which he pointed at them. "You two are in big, big trouble," he bellowed.

"You run," Bart said. "I'll hold them off."

"You'll be massacred," Tessie protested. She grabbed his arm and pulled him with her, away from the mob. "Come with me. Now."

"But…"

"Now." She glared at him and then gave his arm a firm pull. She was not going to have this man's blood on her hands, especially given that it was her fault they were in that situation in the first place.

Bart stared at her and then, realising that she was not going to leave without him, started to run with her.

The men bellowed behind them, which gave extra speed to their legs as they darted down the street and around the first corner, darting this way and that as they tried to lose them.

After a few minutes, Tessie tapped Bart's arm and indicated for him to stop. They stood, listening and staring around, until they were satisfied that they had lost their pursuers.

She smiled triumphantly at Bart until she noticed the look on his face. "What is it?" she asked.

He turned slowly, colour draining from his face. "I've just realised where we are. This is St Giles's."

"Right?" Her understanding of London's geography was limited; she had never really needed to know any place names aside from the names of their hosts at the various parties they attended.

Bart turned wide eyes on her. "We're in the middle of demon territory."

"Oh."

Chapter Fifteen

They hid behind a pile of rubbish in an alleyway, desperately hoping that the demons would not notice them.

In spite of every one of her instincts, Tessie found that she could not tear herself away from the sight before them. She had heard about the creatures, from newspaper articles or scandalous stories told in hushed tones at dinner parties, but she had always assumed that the stories were at best overblown and in all likelihood completely made up.

However, the scene in front of them was straight from those hideous mediaeval church paintings, a picture of hell as imagined by the most imaginative zealot. The creatures filled the street beyond their hiding place, a snarling mass of scaly hides, claws and flashing eyes.

"What do we do?" she whispered.

Bart shrugged. "I could try fighting my way through them. Don't fancy my chances though."

Tessie glanced at him. "You have fought them before?"

"Yeah, but it helps when I've got a weapon. I'm big, but they're bigger."

"Do you think they'll find us hiding here?"

"Nah. They don't tend to be too smart. I reckon they'll move on soon."

She frowned as she looked at the demons, which did not look as though they had any intention of moving at any point. In fact, they seemed to be almost settling down for the day.

"I had never imagined that they would be quite so… ugly," she muttered.

"First time seeing demons?" asked Bart.

"Yes. We were always told that they were inventions of people with rather fevered imaginations. I had read the reports and seen the pictures, but always chose to believe that they were not really real, or at least that they did not belong in my world. To see them in the flesh like this…"

"They're not the least of it," said Bart. "I've seen all sorts; not just demons like this, but there's one big demon who'll give your *nightmares* nightmares. Andras, his name is. Steal your soul as soon as look at you, that one."

"I heard of him," said Tessie, shuddering. "He was the one who brought all the demons down to Earth, wasn't he? Wanting to turn this world into Hell?"

Bart looked at her pale face, wondering if he had gone too far. "Not all of them are bad, though. There's a golem down at Vicky Docks."

"A golem?"

"Yeah. Big thing made out of clay. Ten feet tall and as strong as ten men. He helps out loading and unloading ships."

Tessie shook her head. "Wonders will never cease." She ducked down as one of the demons turned toward them, her heart pounding at the fear of being discovered.

Bart did not seem to be too bothered, though, settling back against the wall. Figuring that there was no point in risking drawing attention to themselves, she shuffled backwards, taking care to not get too close to him. He edged aside to make space for her, looking down awkwardly to avoid looking at her legs.

She looked around at the ramshackle buildings that seemed as though they were ready to fall in on them at any moment. They cast dark shadows on the streets, which was in part a blessing, as it meant that she couldn't see what she was kneeling in. However, it did make her feel more and more claustrophobic as time went by.

She shifted her weight and then shuddered at the squelch from under her feet. "Do people really live in places like this?" she asked.

"Oh yeah," said Bart. "I grew up near here. Wasn't as much demons round here then, but apart from that, not much's changed."

"What, in houses like these?"

He squinted as he looked around. "Not quite. These are a lot posher than what I used to live in. Where I grew up was a bit more cramped together. And the houses didn't have quite so many windows."

"But these have hardly any…" she started, then cleared her throat and asked, "What was it like? Growing up somewhere like this?"

Bart shrugged. "It was fine. Made me what I am today. Taught me plenty."

"Like what?"

"Like how to use my muscle. Always been a big lad. One thing I'm good at, being big."

"Do you take after your father in that respect?" When he looked at her blankly, she added, "Was your father well built, like you?"

He scratched his head. "Couldn't rightly say. Didn't really know me dad. Only me ma. She didn't talk about him, so I never asked."

"Does she still live around here? Your mother?"

Bart looked away. "No," he muttered.

A silence grew between them. Tessie looked around, clearing her throat and wondering what she should say. Then Bart chuckled. "That, over there," he said, gesturing to a patch of land in between two houses. "That's where Spencer and me first met."

"Oh, really?" she asked, staring with feigned interest at the nondescript patch of wasteland.

"Yeah. I remember it like it was yesterday. Must've been twenty years ago or something: I was a lot smaller then, but still bigger than most others my age."

"What age was that?"

He blinked at her. "What age was what?"

"You. How old were you back then?"

"Dunno. I was a kid. I was coming back from doing something—can't remember what—and there was this big group of lads, all stood around cheering and stuff. I went over to see what was going on, and there was this scrawny kid there, being beaten up. Didn't seem fair to me, so I waded in and helped him out."

"That was your friend?"

"Spencer. Yeah. We kind've went from there, never looked back."

"So you have been helping him out ever since?"

He looked at her. "We help each other out. Different skills, you know? Depending on what's needed: brains or muscle."

Tessie flinched at the sound of demons fighting in the street behind them. "How long do you think we should wait?" she asked.

"Dunno, milady. A while. Maybe Spencer'll come and find us; he usually has the ideas."

Tessie frowned. "So you know."

"Know what, milady?"

"That I'm not really a maidservant." She smiled as Bart opened and closed his mouth, struggling to come up with an answer. "It is all right; I suppose you were going to find out sooner or later. I take it that Margaret told you?"

"Who?" frowned Bart.

"The lady who recognised me in the street."

"Oh, no, we didn't talk to her. It was Spencer: he figured it out. He's good like that. Always thinkin' ahead."

She smiled at the expression on his face. "You two are a good team, I take it?"

"He's always been there for me. Lookin' out for me."

"And you look out for him as well."

"Yeah, well, as much as I can. Not really good for much apart from bashin' heads together, me."

"Sometimes that is enough," Tessie pointed out. "Without your intervention just now, I dread to think what would have happened to me."

Bart nodded to the street beyond. "Looks like all I've done is save you from them blokes just so's you can be torn to pieces by demons."

She chuckled, and he looked at her in confusion before grinning.

"I suspect that you put yourself down," said Tessie. "I would imagine that your friend would be lost without you."

"Maybe," said Bart. "But he'd know what to do right now. Probably wouldn't have got us stuck here."

"So what would he have done? If he were here?"

Bart scratched at the top of his head. "Spencer always says if you're in a sticky spot you either run or hide. Trouble is, right now there's nowhere to run that wouldn't be straight into trouble."

"So we wait, just like you said." She thought for a moment and then chuckled.

"What's so funny?"

"If you would have told me this morning that I would have been dressed as a maidservant, hiding in a pile of rubbish with a perfect stranger from a horde of demons, I would have been petrified."

"You don't seem too panicked, milady."

She cocked her head as she thought about this. "It is strange. All of my life I have been told that I was just a weak woman, that I should know my place in the world and not try and deviate from it."

"And what's that, then? Your place?"

"Oh, you know, to follow the wishes of my father, and then when I was married do the same for my husband. To keep a household fit for our place in society, to entertain…" She sighed. "Basically to lead a dull but virtuous life."

"Don't sound much like fun to me."

She smiled. "It does not, does it? I am assured that there are rewards to be gained. That when I have children…" She shuddered.

"I like kids," said Bart. "Always thought I'd have a few of my own at some point."

"You do not have to give birth to them," Tessie pointed out.

"I suppose. Is it so bad, though?"

She stared at him, eyebrows raised and a puzzled smile on her face. "Do you really not…?"

"I dunno. Never really given it much thought."

She opened and then closed her mouth. "Let us just say that I do not relish the impact it would have on my body. And after the birth, it would condemn me to a living hell—there would truly be no escaping my daily torture, of death by stifling boredom."

Bart scratched at his side. "Seems to me that if you feel that way about your life, you should try and change it."

She smiled wearily. "Yes, but how? Everyone just tells me I should stop trying to fight my circumstances, and accept life for the way it is."

"Seems to me like you shouldn't listen to friends like them. There's a big, wide world out here; why don't you just run away?"

She blinked at him. "I could, couldn't I? Yes! Yes, I could! I do not need that life, and maybe I would be happier without it!"

"Sounds to me like you definitely would," said Bart.

"First," she said, drawing herself up to her knees, "we need to make our escape from here. That direction is the way we need to go?"

"Yep. But there's the little matter of all them demons in our way."

Tessie nodded. "We need a distraction," she muttered,

looking up and down the street. She pointed at a house across the way, where dark shadows moved behind a first-floor window. Picking up a brick, she asked Bart, "Could you throw this into that window?"

He hefted the rock, feeling its weight. "Reckon I could," he said. "Why?"

She grinned at him. "Distraction. As soon as you've thrown it, get ready to run."

Bart squatted on one knee, bouncing the brick in his hand as he kept an eye on the window and the demons in the street in front of it. The creatures turned so that they, for a second, had their backs to him and Tessie, and that was the moment he leapt to his feet and launched the brick straight at the window.

They both watched it soar through the air and then smash through the window, throwing themselves down to the ground as the demons turned to look around. Before they could start to investigate where the projectile had come from, other demons started to stream out of the house, glaring at those outside, clearly assuming that they had thrown it. Within moments, the demons were brawling with each other.

"You're right," grinned Tessie. "They really are not very bright. Let's go!" She darted out of their hiding place and around the corner, Bart lumbering in her wake.

*

They collapsed against a wall, chuckling as they fought to get their breaths back.

"Have we lost them?" Tessie asked.

"Don't think they ever clocked we was there in the first place," said Bart.

"There you are," said Spencer, darting round the corner and glaring at them. "I've been lookin' all over for you."

"Sorry," said Bart. "We got trapped in St Giles. Stuck hiding from a load of demons. Would've been there still if it weren't for

Tessie here."

She shook her head. "It was all thanks to your throwing arm; I would never have been able to make the distraction without you."

"Still your idea though," grinned Bart, his chest swelling with pride, making him look as though he had grown ten feet.

Spencer frowned from one to the other. "Well, you're here now. We'd better get you back before your…ah…employer misses you."

"It's all right," said Bart. "She knows we know."

"Know what?"

"That I am not really a maidservant," she said. "That I'm actually Lady Marchant."

Spencer put his hands on his hips. "Well I'm glad you two've had so much time to get to know each other," he said. "But now we need to get you back to your house."

Tessie shook her head. "I am not going back."

"Beg pardon?"

"I had a good conversation with Bart," she said. "He made me realise a lot of things. My life is not a life worth living. I am going to run away."

Spencer glared at Bart and then turned to face her. "Just like that? You have some money saved up, I take it?"

She shook her head defiantly. "I will make my own way."

Spencer laughed in disbelief. "You will make your own way. I take it your husband controls all your family money. So if you run away, you get nothing."

"I will make my own way," she said again, shrugging.

"So you've got some magic way of making money then?"

She glared back at him, while Bart grabbed his arm and pulled him away.

"What's the matter with you?" Bart asked him.

"I could ask you the same thing! What're you doin', putting ideas in her head like that?"

"She's not happy right now. Seems like the best thing she can do is to leave all that behind, right?"

"And how's she going to afford to live, without her big house and all that lovely money, eh? More to the point, how's she going to afford to pay us?"

"Oh," said Bart. "I didn't think."

"No, you didn't. And as usual, it's up to me to fix things." He turned and marched towards Tessie. "You want to see what it's like, making your own way out here on the streets? Come with me."

He led them down a series of run-down streets, dodging dirty children and leering groups of men and women. The stench of unwashed bodies grew until it was almost overwhelming, until they came to an intersection of seven streets, all meeting in a central point like spokes of a dark, dirty, run-down wheel. "Welcome to Seven Dials," said Spencer, holding out his arms to gesture around at the seething mass of bodies shouting and barging as they went about their daily business around them. His arm caught one man in the chest and Spencer had to do some quick apologising to fend off a fight. The man only accepted the apology when he saw Bart glowering over his shoulder.

Tessie looked around, discomfited by the sheer numbers pressing around her as well as the casual boisterousness with which they conducted themselves. While she was used to being around a mix of people in the crowded streets of London, she was not used to so many of the lower classes together in one area, all at home in a place where she clearly had no hope of ever belonging.

"See her over there?" Spencer asked, pointing to a woman who was weaving between and around the stalls and barrows, a basket of flowers in her arms. "She's up before dawn each day to gather her wares, then spends all day on her feet floggin' them to anyone who'll take them. The trick's to get rid before the day gets too old and the wares get worth less. Most of what she earns goes to buyin' more flowers the next day; she'll take home a few pennies which she needs to spend on food and lodgings for her whole family. Same goes for most of the girls out here.

"Or maybe you fancy somethin' indoors? See that house there? Probably ten rooms in there, each of them'll have at least one family apiece in there."

"Each room?" Tessie asked.

"Yeah, each room. Not big rooms either—probably about as big as from here to that wall. And by 'family' I don't mean just a husband and wife; I also mean their kids, grandparents, you name it. Probably four or five to a bed, ten or so to a room. But during the day, if you're lucky, you could earn some coin by unpicking clothes, or sewing or suchlike."

"I could sew," Tessie pointed out.

"Not your fancy needlepoint," said Spencer. "You get paid by the piece, and what you get paid is next to nothing. So you do a lot of sewing, all day and all night, to earn a couple of pennies to pay your way."

"Every day?"

"Yes, every day. You need to take a day off, you don't earn, you go hungry. Of course, there're factories you could work in: matchstick factories, say. That's where this lady here works. Afternoon, Angie."

A woman turned to nod and then moved on, leaving Tessie staring at her.

"Her mouth... What happened to her face?"

"Oh yeah, occupational hazard. You see, the stuff they put in matches don't mix too well with people. It gets under their skin, rots them away. Angie was at the matchstick factory six months afore her jaw dropped right off, rotted away. 'Phossy jaw', they call it."

Tessie had a hand over her mouth, the colour draining from her cheeks. "I thought they were just tales..."

"Shall we see what else you could do? The dye shops, where you'll be wading in piss all day? Or maybe you could make a living lying on your back at night..."

"That's enough," said Bart.

"And that's all before we think about what could happen to you when you're not tryin' to earn coin. Like when you're walkin' the streets at night all alone and some blokes take a liking to you. Maybe they're nasty drunken types. Maybe they're the Tappers…"

"Tappers?" she asked. "But that's not a real thing, surely?"

"Ladies keep going missing," said Spencer. "And the one common thing everyone agrees on is that these Tappers are involved. And the ladies are never seen again. You fancyin' becoming another one of them, eh?"

"That's enough," said Bart again, louder.

Spencer took a deep breath and noticed that Tessie was staring around wide-eyed. "So maybe you'll agree now, milady," he said in a softer voice, "that we should get you back home."

She nodded, wiping the tears from her eyes.

*

"I'm not happy about this," grumbled Bart as they walked behind Tessie.

"It's the best thing for her," said Spencer.

"Best thing for *us*, you mean. Best way for us to get paid."

"No. Well, yes. But the likes of her don't know how to make their own way. Trust me: she'd not last longer than a few days. You know what it's like out there for a streetwise girl; imagine what it'd be like for her. If the Tappers are stalkin' the streets, they'll snap her up in no time, and she'll never be seen again. This is better for her, trust me. And we can help her better if her husband don't suspect nothing. We keep an eye on her, make sure she don't come to no harm. All right?"

"I suppose…"

Tessie slowed her pace and turned to them. "That's my street there. My house is number fifteen."

"We'll come with you and keep watch," said Bart. "Make sure you don't come to no harm."

Tessie smiled briefly at him and then shook her head. "It is best that he does not suspect anything. If he were to see me socialising with yourselves, he is going to get suspicious."

"Quite right, miss," said Spencer. "Don't worry; we'll be discreet."

She levelled a long hard stare at him and then turned. "Our deal still stands," she said over her shoulder. "I expect you to help me solve my predicament. I want to know exactly what my husband is up to. No more money until then."

They watched as she turned and walked away, her poise once again transformed into that of a self-assured noblewoman.

"Bitch," muttered Spencer. "After all we did, she still talks to us like we're no more than street rubbish."

"All *I* did, you mean," said Bart. "You just made her feel bad."

"For the last time: I talked sense into her…!" Spencer shook his head. "Never mind. Come on, let's go. Keep a careful distance; after all, wouldn't want her ladyship to think she might mix with the likes of us, eh?"

He walked in the direction of the house, Bart in his wake.

Chapter Sixteen

Tessie stepped through her front door, her heart in her mouth.

"Your husband's waiting for you," said the butler, his expression unreadable as he looked her up and down. "Waiting for you in the front parlour, I believe. He asked that you see him as soon as you returned."

She smiled in a way that she hoped was natural but feared looked overly nervous. "Thank you." She suddenly realised she was still dressed in the borrowed clothes which had formed her failed maidservant disguise. "I will be with him shortly," she said. "I just need to freshen up."

She made her way up the stairs to her room, ignoring the man's sardonic comment of "Indeed, ma'am". A few minutes later she re-emerged, more suitably dressed although even more flustered than before.

The walk down the hall to the front parlour door seemed to take forever, the sounds of the clock and her heels on the floor ringing loud in her ears. She tried to steady her breathing and, as she reached out to open the door, she was dismayed to see her hand shaking.

With one last deep breath, she stepped into the room to see her husband silhouetted against the window.

"Where have you been?" he asked, not bothering to turn round to address her.

"Johnson's. And then I took a walk to clear my head. And where have you been?"

She instantly regretted biting back at him as he spun round, his eyes flashing with venom. "I do not recall needing to account for myself to you," he snapped. He looked her up and down. "You have changed clothes. I watched you come in: dressed like a common washerwoman."

"You have never before expressed any interest in how I look," she snapped. "I wonder if this has anything to do with that masquerade at the séance the other night. I would prefer if you kept yourself out of my business and I shall keep out of yours. Now, if that is all…" She turned and stormed out before he could respond, her heart in her mouth, scarcely believing that she had finally spoken to him in that way. Maybe it was the confidence in knowing she now had someone on her side—however unconventional they might be—or simply the culmination of all those months and years of mistreatment.

Regardless, while she feared what consequences may follow, she could not help but smile broadly as she marched back upstairs.

*

Marchant watched her walk out of the room, clenching and unclenching his fists, stunned into silence by the woman's sheer impudence. By the time he had recovered enough of his wits to even think of a response, she was up the stairs. He contemplated following and showing her what happened to women who spoke to him in that manner, but then shook his head. A bit of feistiness was no bad thing, he reminded himself, for what they had planned.

He turned back to the window and glared outside. After a moment, he bellowed, "Cummings!" The butler was at his side in no time at all.

"Sir?" the man asked.

"Those two rough-looking fellows out there," Marchant said. "Over the road. They have not stopped staring at this house for the past few minutes."

"I see them, sir," said Cummings. "Would you like me to, ahem, encourage them to leave?"

"Yes. Very much so. In as forceful a manner as possible." He allowed himself a brief smile as Cummings nodded and departed. He would enjoy this little sideshow. Then he frowned. "I recognise you two…"

Chapter Seventeen

Spencer shifted his position in their cramped hiding place, deliberately elbowing Bart in the chest and then ignoring his protests.

"Shush. He's coming out."

Ever since they had been chased away by a surprisingly well-armed group of Marchant's servants, they had been forced to hide in the bushes a little way down the street. The humiliation of skulking around like that was much more preferable to being beaten and chased by Marchant's thugs; the experience had simply strengthened Spencer's desire to get Marchant. It wasn't just about the money now: it was personal.

Although, if he was totally honest, it was still mainly about the money.

They squatted down lower as they watched Marchant step out of his front door, look around, and then make his way in the direction of the City.

Both men extracted themselves from the foliage, grunting and swearing, and then followed at a safe distance, brushing themselves down in a vain attempt to look at least partway presentable.

At the corner, Marchant hailed a Hackney Carriage, forcing them to break into a light jog to keep up. Thankfully the sheer volume of traffic on the roads—not only other vehicles but also pedestrians—meant that the carriage was not able to pull too far ahead, and Spencer and Bart did not have to work too hard to keep pace.

They slowed down and took cover behind a stall as the carriage came to a stop outside a tall building on Threadneedle Street. Marchant stepped out and, with a glance around, walked into the building.

"What's it say above the door?" asked Bart.

Spencer frowned. "The Thau-ma-tur-gical Society." He picked over the unfamiliar combination of lettering slowly.

"What's that mean? It foreign or somethin'?"

"Must be. Dunno. I've heard of that somewhere before, though."

They settled down to wait, taking care this time not to linger within direct sight of the building's windows.

Costermongers called their wares, and carriage drivers swung their crops and shouted abuse at those pedestrians who would not get out of their way in time, attracting responses in kind from those on foot. The well-heeled picked their way around the edges of this chaos, women clinging onto their mens' arms for dear life while affecting an air of not noticing the riff-raff which surrounded them. Drawn to all of this were those who made their livings from the scraps, the street children and petty crooks who spent their waking hours trying to blend into the background, to avoid getting caught as they lifted money from pockets and jewellery from unsuspecting owners.

All of this was second nature to Spencer and Bart, the rhythm by which they lived their lives. They were immune to the intolerably loud noise in the street, their senses having been dulled by a lifetime of scenes like this.

"He's takin' his time," remarked Spencer after a while, if only to break the boredom.

Bart grunted. "Must be an important meetin'."

Spencer walked over to a nearby stall. "Oi, mate, what's that buildin' over there?"

The stallholder looked Spencer up and down, ready to berate him for wasting his time. Then he registered the huge figure looming behind him and decided that some manners probably wouldn't cost him much, after all.

"That place?" said the stallholder. "Set up just the other week, with a new fancy sign an' all. Don't know what they do, but they don't buy or sell out here, that's for sure. Load of folks in suits come and go, but they don't stop to bother us out here, so I keep myself to my own business. Safest way."

Spencer frowned. "Safe? What do you mean?"

"Just that," blinked the man, turning back to his stall and non-existent customers.

"Just that that's a pretty strange set of words to use when talking about a normal buildin', don't you think?" pressed Spencer. "If we were stood here talkin' about a bank or an office, you'd not say it were safest way to not bother about them. But if we were talkin' about some place run by a gang boss, well… That's another matter, ain't it?"

The man glanced around. "Look, I don't know who you are, but I don't bother myself with that place. It's not there, far as I'm concerned, and you can tell whoever you're workin' for I said that. I've got a family to feed; I don't need no trouble. But if you're askin' out of general curiosity, then my advice to you is to leave well alone, you hear?"

"Is it me, or did that seem a bit odd?" asked Bart as they walked away.

"Somethin's not right, that's for sure," muttered Spencer. "Which just makes me think…"

"That we should find out what that Lord bloke is up to, before he puts 'er Ladyship in any more danger!" finished Bart with a grin, walking back over to the wall on the other side of the street to continue his watching vigil.

"Wasn't quite what I had in mind," muttered Spencer, shaking his head as he slowly followed.

They stopped short as they saw the two policemen walking towards them. "Run?" asked Bart.

"Nah," said Spencer. "We've done nothing wrong."

They stood and waited for the policemen to reach them. "Afternoon boys," said PC Jones. "What are you two up to?"

"Nothing dodgy, if that's what you're thinkin'," said Spencer.

"Really." The policeman regarded them suspiciously. "And if we were to search you?"

"You'd find nothing illegal. We're reformed characters, us."

PC Jones looked at his colleague and then shrugged. "You just be aware: we're keeping an eye on you two."

*

After a couple of hours, hunger and thirst got the better of even Bart's sense of duty. Spencer pointed out a pub from which they would still be able to keep an eye on the building's door while getting a pie and pint and, as a light rain started to fall, Bart agreed.

The pub was narrow and cramped, with a handful of rough wooden tables dotted around the walls. One table sat against the window to the street, which was decorated with coloured panes of glass to protect the privacy of customers from the prying eyes of spouses or employers. The table was occupied by two grimy faced men, who looked up as Spencer and Bart approached.

"'Scuse us," said Spencer. "But my friend here really likes this window, and it'd really ruin his drinkin' if he couldn't sit 'ere and admire it."

The men glared at him, expressions which softened into wide-eyed paleness as Bart appeared in front of them. They stood quickly and darted away, leaving the table free.

"That was kind of them," grinned Spencer, waving a hand to catch the barmaid's eye. "Two ales please, and two meat pies," he said as she sullenly approached.

"Show me your coin first," she said. "No offence, but we've

'ad enough time wasters this week, and my pay gets docked if you do a runner."

Spencer tutted and spread a handful of coins on the table. "Disgraceful. Whatever is happenin' to the world, eh?"

As the barmaid walked away, a dark figure appeared at their table, sliding onto the bench next to Spencer. "I see you've been busy," said Thaddeus. "Let me save you the time of going all the way to Milton to give him your share." He held out his hand.

Spencer pursed his lips as he reached into his pocket and pulled out a handful of coins, counting them into Thaddeus's hand.

"That's his cut," he said, after the magician's hand was full of money.

"And…" said Thaddeus.

Spencer shook his head. "It's like you can't trust anyone these days." He handed over a few more coins.

"Good man," said Thaddeus. "So what are you two up to now?"

"We're doing a job for some toff. She wants us to find out what her husband's up to."

"That's where this cash came from? Lucrative job." He waved a hand at the barmaid and a moment later a mug of beer was in front of him. "He's paying," he said, gesturing to Spencer. When Spencer hesitated, he added, "I'm sure you want to keep on my good side, don't you…"

Spencer grumbled as he tossed a coin at the barmaid. "Could we have ours as well, if that's not too much trouble?" he asked.

She glared at him and then walked away, returning a few moments later with two mugs of beer, which she slammed on the table.

"Thanks," muttered Spencer, wiping away the beer which had slopped onto the table. "So what's your story?" he asked Thaddeus. "How come you ended up working for Milton."

Thaddeus paused mid drink. "I do not work for that man," he said.

"Could've fooled me."

"It is a temporary arrangement," Thaddeus continued, through gritted teeth.

"Ah," nodded Spencer. "One of them."

"What do you mean, 'one of them'?" Thaddeus put down his drink and turned his head to stare at him.

"I mean one of them sort of arrangements. What is it? Paying off a debt? That's usually what it is."

"Something like that." Thaddeus turned back to his drink.

Spencer eyed him for a moment, a smile playing on his lips. "'Course, it's a big honour to be working for someone like Milton, ain't it?"

"I'm not…" he stopped himself, hands gripping the mug a little too tight. "I would not normally deal with the likes of him."

"Yeah, he is a tough one, I'll give you that. Most folk struggle to get that close to him: professionally, you know?"

"That was a clever trick you pulled, back at Milton's," said Bart. "You know, what you did to Nicky. How'd you do that? Something to do with demons?"

"I do not stoop to play with demonic possessions, if that's what you're asking," said Thaddeus. "There are degrees of magical arts: I practice the higher arts. And be careful with your language; I am not some parlour illusionist, playing 'tricks' on people. I follow the purest forms of magic."

"Didn't look that pure, what you did to Nicky," observed Spencer. "Looked downright nasty. We saw him the other day, didn't we, Bart? Poor bloke's a gibbering wreck. Just sat there in the street, not eating, not caring about anything."

"Then the magic has done its work."

"How's about you stop it?" asked Bart. "You know, lift the spell or whatever it is."

"Why?" asked Thaddeus.

"Because… He's learnt his lesson?"

"Who'd pay me to do it?"

"But…" Bart blinked. "It's kind of not nice?"

Thaddeus laughed. "I thought you two were tough street criminals. Since when did you bother yourselves with what is 'nice'?"

Spencer shrugged. "S'pose you've got a point. And anyway, if you did lift it, you'd have Milton upset with you. Wouldn't want that, would you?"

"That is the least of my worries," Thaddeus spat. "I am not afraid of him."

"Here," said Bart. "If you do magic, you use magic books, right?"

Thaddeus shuddered. "We do not refer to them as 'magic books', but yes."

"Was it you that Seth stole that book for? No, hang on, that's not right: it was that other bloke he sold it to, wasn't it?"

"Yeah," said Spencer. "You got a partner then?"

Thaddeus stared at him. "I work alone. What book was it you stole?"

"*Seth* stole. You know Seth: big bald-headed bloke, works for Milton as well."

"I know who he is. What book was it?"

"Big thing. Red, it was."

"What was the title?"

"Dunno," said Spencer. "Didn't have a chance to look that close."

"You can read, can you?"

"Of course! Just need a bit of time to make sure I've got the words right, and it wasn't in front of me for long enough. It had some sort of picture on the cover though. What was it?"

"Big scary thing," said Bart. "Horns and stuff. A goat?"

"Not a goat! Goats ain't scary."

"A devil?" asked Thaddeus.

Spencer snapped his fingers. "Yes! That's it: a devil."

Thaddeus stood up and stormed out of the pub.

"What's up with him?" asked Bart.

"I think Seth's about to get a little visit from a very upset magician," chuckled Spencer.

*

A little while later, the barmaid plonked two plates of unappetising-looking food on the table. "'Ere, your friend: he all right?" she asked.

Spencer looked over at Bart, who was staring intently through one of the lighter panes of glass, his nose practically pushed up against it.

"Yeah, he's fine. Just likes stained glass windows. You should see 'im in churches: can never get 'im out!"

She nodded slowly before turning to walk away.

"Actually," said Spencer, stopping her in her tracks, "you could settle an argument we're 'avin'. That building over yonder with the long posh name: Thauma-thingy Society. My mate reckons it's a bank, but I'm sure it's some government thing. You know?"

She looked from one of them to the other, peering at them to try and work out whether this was some form of test. Having satisfied herself that no spy, no matter how good, would ever be able to look quite so appallingly incompetent, she lent toward them.

"I'd not ask too many questions if I were you. Couldn't tell you what they did, but there are some strange comin's and goin's in that building."

"What do you mean?"

"We used to have a medium who'd come in here regular, like: do readin's for customers, all that stuff. Then the other day she's approached by a man from that place over there, and we don't see 'er no more. Turns out she's gone to work for them. My boss did his nut—she were a good earner for us, drawin' in punters and keepin' them drinkin' while they waited their turn. I hear other pubs've had the same problem; since that place set up, it's been suckin' up all the mediums and spirit readers and the like and gettin' them to work there."

"Doing what?" asked Spencer.

"No idea. Bloke was in here other night, askin' round for people to do fetchin' and carryin' work for them. Seem to be payin' good wages, so you can see why the mediums'd prefer to work over there. Still pretty strange, though. Even these days: why'd you want so many spiritual people?"

"Anyone else go in there?" asked Bart. "Young girls, or demons?"

She frowned at him. "I don't know," she said slowly, "I don't keep a constant watch on there. Got a job to do. Who are you two anyway? Why'd you want to know?"

"We're nobody," said Spencer quickly, glaring at Bart to keep quiet. "Like I said, just wonderin'."

"Yeah, well, you be careful. Folks who wonder stuff, tend to get themselves killed." She walked back to the bar, clearly keen to get as much space as possible between her and these curious customers.

"Well, you know what that means," said Bart.

"That we should definitely leave well alone and just give up? Take the coin milady's given us so far and be grateful we only escaped with a mild beating?" offered Spencer in a hopeful voice.

"We should go and ask about gettin' some work over there, find out what they're doin' and what our Lord bloke's got to do with it."

Spencer rubbed his temples with the tips of his fingers. "Don't suppose there's any point in me tryin' to persuade you otherwise, is there?"

"Nope," grinned Bart through a mouthful of pie.

Spencer sighed and then shrugged. "I s'pose if we're careful, keep ourselves out the way, we could earn some extra coin here. At least earn back all that food you're stuffing your face with. For the record though, I reckon this is a very very stupid idea."

Bart grinned, pointing at his friend's part-eaten pie. "You finished with that?"

Chapter Eighteen

Spencer had hoped that, if his persuasive powers couldn't convince Bart of the stupidity of trying to get work at The Thaumaturgical Society, then they would at least be saved from making fools of themselves by their complete lack of any useful experience or skills.

"Yes, we still have vacancies," beamed a face from the doorway. "Come in, come in!"

The two men glanced at each other and, before Spencer could try one last attempt at convincing Bart to see sense, they were inside the building.

They found themselves in a long, wide corridor which was lined with oak panelling and caked in cobwebs. The hall was lined with packing crates and sheets covering odd-shaped objects, while the air was thick with dust which assailed their lungs as well as played lazily in the sparse light from the few lanterns dotted around.

"Nice," muttered Spencer as they followed the man down the hallway. "Not had a chance to move in yet, eh?"

"We have been rather more preoccupied with the business at hand to worry ourselves about cleaning and tidying," said the man, striding ahead of them. "But also hampered by the lack of available willing labour. Wait in here and someone will be with you shortly."

They found themselves in a room which was only slightly less dirty and cluttered than the hall outside, with packing boxes taking the place of furniture and indeed obscuring much of the floor and walls. Spencer paced the room, trying to find any other exit and reassure himself that there were no hidden traps waiting to be sprung on them. Bart sat down on a crate and settled for just staring at the door while humming to himself.

"You're not even the smallest bit worried, are you?" snapped Spencer.

"Worried? About what? We're gettin' a job. You said you wanted to go straight. No better way than this, right?"

Spencer marched over to him, dropping his voice to a whisper. "You saw the way them folks out there spoke about this place. Somethin's not right here; you must see that."

"That's why we're here. If that Lord bloke's mixed up in somethin', his wife needs to know."

"And that's the other thing—"

"His wife. Our *client*," Bart reminded him.

"Yes, yes," continued Spencer. "But what if that Lord bloke sees us here? What then?"

Bart frowned. "But he's gone. We watched him go just before we came here."

"And if he comes back? He knows what we look like; he sent his man after us not that long ago. If he comes here and recognises us, we'd be done for."

"We just say it were a big misunderstandin'," shrugged Bart. "No law against us being outside his house. And then it were just chance that we ended up workin' here."

Spencer ran his fingers through his hair. "Please, let's just go. Right now. We can tell the folks here we're no longer interested and—"

He was interrupted by the door swinging open to reveal a large, thick-set man who had been squeezed awkwardly into a dark suit. He frowned at them over a bushy beard which appeared to have resisted all attempts to be brushed into a civilised fashion.

"You the two come about a job?" he asked in a low rumble.

"Yeah," said Bart, jumping to his feet. Spencer took a deep breath and tried to arrange his face into an innocent expression.

"I know you two, don't I?" the man looked from one to the other of them.

"Not likely," Spencer said quickly. "We're new in these parts, just passing through, lookin' for work. Of course, if there's none for us then—"

"You used to work for Jason Simmons, back in St Giles'. Few years back. I remember you. Can hardly miss you, the way you two look."

"That's us," grinned Bart as Spencer groaned inwardly.

"So what you doin' round this part of town?"

"Jason got sent down, didn't he?" Spencer said, before Bart could drop them in more trouble by saying anything dangerous or stupid, like the truth. "We've been doin' bits here and there, but now we're lookin' to go straight. Fed up with always lookin' over our shoulders, not to mention starvin' all the time."

The man glared at them. Spencer tried to keep from looking away, forcing himself to meet the man's stare. He tried to empty his mind, in case his thoughts were written in his eyes, but the more he tried the more his doubts and fears bubbled to the surface. Bart had no such issues, though: staring back with wide-eyed innocence.

The man grunted. "You'll be in my gang. I'll be keepin' a close eye on you; I don't take with no trouble in my gang, you hear? Keep your noses clean, do as you're told, you'll get half-a-bob a piece at the end of the week."

Spencer blinked. "Half-a-bob? As in ten shillings? A week?"

"You can do sums," the man growled. "You want a prize or somethin'? That's the pay, take it or leave it. You know where the door is."

Spencer was so preoccupied with the thought of a regular

income of that size that he completely missed the opportunity to run. Before he could react, Bart had stepped forward, his hand outstretched. "We'll take it, please an' thank you."

The man stared at the huge slab of meat which passed for Bart's hand and then shook it, trying not to wince as the other man squeezed in a handshake firm enough to crack knuckles and bones.

"You got names?" the man asked as he shook Spencer's hand.

"I'm Spencer, this is Bart. What about you? What do we call you?"

"You call me Mr Davis. Now come this way; we've got a bit of liftin' and carryin' to be done." He glanced at Spencer. "You up for that? I know your mate'll be all right, but I won't have people not doin' their fair share."

"I'm stronger than I look," Spencer said, his cheeks reddening. "I can do my bit."

They stepped out into a courtyard at the rear of the house, which was filled with six-foot-high stacks of crates. "All these need to go up to the third floor," said the man. "Grab one and follow me and I'll show you where. And be careful; there's delicate stuff in them and if any are broken, we'll dock your pay."

Each crate was four feet square and all seemed identical, save for markings in red paint on their sides. Spencer made a show of not looking at the markings, an instinct born of a lifetime avoiding seeing anything which might get him in trouble. While Bart would have been able to take the weight of each crate on his own, their size meant that he needed Spencer's help and so they took either end of the nearest one, following Mr Davis into the house and wincing at the jingling noises coming from within their load.

"What's this stuff?" asked Spencer. "Some sort of glass?"

"There's the other thing," said Mr Davis. "Keep your heads down and don't ask questions. Our employers appreciate people who keep their noses out of their business, understand? Just do as you're told, and you'll collect your coin at the end of the week.

That clear?"

"Just makin' conversation," muttered Spencer.

"Don't. Head down, don't ask questions, don't poke your nose around anywhere. Some folks who've forgotten that, they've lived to regret it. And I don't just mean missin' out on half-a-bob a week, neither." He turned a hard stare on them both. "Understand?"

They nodded and started up the stairs after him, taking care to try and keep the crate as level as they could. Spencer shot a glare at his friend, trying to convey through his expression the need for them to be shot of the place as soon as they could. Bart grinned back at him, oblivious.

The first staircase led to a short landing and then up another narrow staircase, the crate scraping noisily against the walls as they went. Spencer reflected that their job would be a lot easier if they were allowed to use the main stairs, rather than the servants' backstairs, but he knew better than to press this with their new boss. The more he saw them as troublemakers, or people with ideas, the more likely they were to end up in some sort of trouble. Old instincts kicked in, honed by the lessons of hundreds of beatings and near-misses. Keep your head down, make yourself as invisible as possible, and no one, particularly not the toffs, would ever notice you. That was the safest way.

They reached the top landing and, breathing heavily from the effort, were relieved to be led to a large room. "Put it there, in the far corner," said Mr Davis. "You'll be filling this room up with all them crates outside, so make sure you stack them starting from the far side. And leave space in between so people can get at the stuff inside. That all clear? Good. You can find your way down and back here all right? Good. Remember what I said: keep your heads down and don't ask questions. I'll be back to check on you later."

"What if we're finished before you come back?" asked Spencer.

The man stared at him and then burst into laughter. "You manage that, you can 'ave a nice long rest out there in the yard.

But you don't go wandering anywhere else looking for me; understand?"

"Crystal," said Spencer. "Right, Bart?"

"Right," said Bart.

*

Spencer relaxed as he realised that their work kept them in the backstairs, with the servants, and so was highly unlikely to bring them into contact with any of the toffs or their visitors. He almost found himself enjoying the work, seeing a kind of righteous release in the hard toil. For the first few hours they kept their heads down and did as they were told, taking satisfaction in seeing the upstairs room fill up and the yard outside slowly empty.

Curiosity started to get the better of Bart, though. "What's that noise, you think?" he whispered, stopping by a door on the middle landing on their way downstairs.

"None of our business, that's what," Spencer hissed, continuing on past him to the next set of stairs.

"Sounds like moanin', like someone's in pain or somethin'."

"Better them than us," muttered Spencer, pausing at the top of the stairs before reluctantly walking back over. He listened at the door for a moment and then shook his head. "Could be anythin'. Let's go."

"But we're supposed to be findin' stuff out," protested Bart as they made their way down the stairs.

"No, we're supposed to be stayin' alive and earnin' money. We do as we're told, remember?"

"But that Lord bloke could be doin' who-knows-what, while we're stuck here moving crates around," said Bart. "Maybe this was a bad idea."

Spencer let out a short, high-pitched giggle. "You think? So now you agree with me? How about we cut our losses and run while we still can?"

"No. Somethin's not right about this place, and if that Lord's mixed up in it then, well, that might be somethin'."

"We're goin' to risk our necks on a feelin' now, are we?"

"The Lady said she was worried about séances and stuff like that. The word out there was that there was mediums being brought in 'ere to do who-knows-what. That's a connection, ain't it?"

Spencer shook his head. "That's a load of gossip and rumour, that's all. There's nothin' here, mark my words."

"We don't even know what this place does," said Bart. "Thauma— what did you say it was called?"

"Thaumaturgical Society," said Spencer, walking over to the nearest crate, leaning against it and then jumping back as it shifted to the side under his weight.

"What's that even mean?" Bart asked. "It foreign or somethin'?"

"Probably. Sounds a bit like 'metal'; maybe they do some sort of smelting or somethin'."

Bart stared at him. "Thought you were supposed to be the smart one? Where you seen a smelting plant in here?"

"I dunno," muttered Spencer, staring at the crate which had been revealed by his leaning on the one above it. "Maybe this is just a place for packin' and sellin' stuff they make somewhere else."

"What about them red markings on the side of the crates? Do they tell us anything?"

"They're just random numbers and letters; probably some sort of code so they know what's in each crate. I tell you, we're wastin' our—" He slid the crate back a bit further and then frowned at the lettering revealed underneath.

"What is it?" asked Bart.

"Looks like Thaumaturgical Society ain't the full title of this place," said Spencer slowly. "Says here these are to be delivered to this address, care of The Thaumaturgical and Paranormal Research Society. Ah."

Bart looked up at him with a wide-eyed grin. "Paranormal? As in…?"

"Ghosts and demons and mediums and spirits and stuff," said Spencer. "Bugger."

Chapter Nineteen

B art pried open a couple of crates to see what was inside. "Just jars and tubes and stuff," he muttered.

"You can't—" stammered Spencer. "What if they find out?"

"How they goin' to do that?" asked Bart, hammering the nails back in place with his fist. "Keep watch and let me know if anyone comes."

Spencer shook his head, muttering to himself. Up until that point he had been happy to convince himself that it was in the girl's best interests to not know what her husband was up to, that he was just another one of them toffs who played around behind his wife's back; something she might be better off not knowing about.

But he had to admit that there was something about that place which did not quite feel right, and to have the proof in black-and-white that they were doing something with the paranormal… Well, that tied in far too closely with what he had assumed were just her paranoid fears. But now it looked like it wasn't just paranoia; after all, they'd written it on a sign, as a part of an official society name. Spencer didn't know much about the workings of business and high society, but he knew that putting things in letters gave them meaning. You couldn't just write any old thing on a sign; if you wrote something down and showed it to the world, that meant something. In this case, it meant that they were serious about doing research into the paranormal and whatever that other thing was. He had seen far too much of what dabbling in the paranormal could do to just dismiss all of this and abandon Lady Marchant to whatever fate had in store for her. Then again, he also had a responsibility to himself and Bart: to make sure that they didn't suffer such a fate either.

"You know what," he said, the thought striking him like a ray of sunshine. "You're right, Bart. We can't just leave the girl to suffer whatever it is they might be doin' here. We should go and tell someone. There're people who deal with this sort of stuff. We should tell them, and they can deal with all this."

"Yeah," said Bart. "But you think they'd listen to us?"

"Of course they would," said Spencer slowly, trying to convince himself as well as Bart, and failing on both counts.

"We need proof," said Bart, shaking his head. "That's what they always say, ain't it? 'Show me the proof.' We need to get proof." He hammered the lid back down on the crate he had just been peering into and then moved to one side of it. "Come on."

"What?"

"Let's take this inside, and then see what we can find while we're in there."

*

"I don't like this," whispered Spencer as they made their way along the landing to the first room. "It ain't our place to be doin' this. We should get the real experts in."

Bart paused outside the door and then turned to him. "All right," he whispered. "You're the brains. So tell me this: what we goin' to tell them?"

"That there's this society up to no good, and they need to stop them."

"And when they ask us how we know this, what we gonna say?"

"Because… The name… Which is up on the door in plain sight… All right, not that. But then there's all the mediums bein' taken in here."

"We've not seen any of them yet though, have we? And we

don't know there's actually bad stuff happening here, do we?"

"No…" Spencer frowned. All they had was rumour and vague feelings, which wouldn't be enough to convince anyone. "Shit," he muttered again. "All right, you win. Just be careful."

Bart flashed him a triumphant grin and then turned back to the door, turning the handle slowly. "It's locked," he mouthed, stepping back and gesturing to his friend.

Spencer glared at him for a moment and then produced his lockpick from his sleeve. "Time was, I used to be the one givin' the orders," he muttered under his breath. "Then he gets himself all besotted with some toff woman and suddenly we're goin' straight into trouble rather than running away, which would be the much more sensible way of doin' things." The lock clicked open after a few seconds and he stepped aside, the lockpick disappearing back into his clothing once more.

Bart turned the handle and gently edged the door open.

At first, they thought that the room was empty, but as their eyes adjusted to the gloom, they could make out a figure sat in a chair in the middle of the floor. It was an old lady dressed in shabby clothes, her head covered by a dark shawl. She was unmoving, her attention focused on the far wall.

"She all right, you reckon?" Bart whispered.

Spencer was about to reply when something flickered across the room. Before he could dismiss it as a trick of the light or his imagination, it reappeared, whirling round the old lady's head. It was a faint white sheet, trailing pale tendrils in its wake so it almost looked like it was wrapping threads around her. They watched, spellbound, as it looped this way and that before it seemed to notice them and twisted in their direction. Quickly, Bart shut the door.

"What the…?" he managed.

Spencer's ears pricked at a noise from below. "Someone coming," he hissed.

They started down the stairs, assuming the air of incurious workers once more. Mr Davis appeared round the corner. "There you are," he said. "I've been looking for you." Before they could say anything, he added, "Got another job for you. Come on, you can finish with the crates later."

They followed him to the bottom of the stairs and then round towards the front of the house, where a black carriage was waiting.

"Get on the sides," said Mr Davis. "We're going to collect someone and need you two to look nice and menacing, just in case anything should happen."

"What sort of thing might happen?" asked Spencer.

"What did I tell you about asking questions? Jump on and hold on tight. We're not going far."

Mr Davis climbed into the carriage while Spencer and Bart jumped up onto the steps on either side and grabbed hold of the handrails. Through the window, Spencer caught a glimpse of another figure inside the vehicle, a well-dressed man who glanced coldly at Mr Davis before banging the head of his cane on the carriage's roof. The driver shook the reins and they moved off, Spencer and Bart holding on tightly as they jerked and swayed along the road.

Bart was mouthing questions at him and, while Spencer could not understand the exact words, he knew the gist of what he was trying to say. He shook his head and nodded down to the carriage roof. Anything they said would be heard by the two men inside; best to save any conversation until they knew they were alone.

His head reeled with questions, though, and the possible answers which sprang from those questions made him feel sick to the pit of his stomach. They were out of their depth in every single way. This was not the way he had planned things; they were supposed to be steering clear of danger, not wading straight into it. Especially trouble of this kind; all his experiences of the paranormal had convinced him that that was a world he wanted to keep as far away from as possible.

He looked over at Bart, at the innocent mountain of a man,

staring around without a care in the world. He blamed himself; he was supposed to keep his friend safe and yet he had allowed him to head off on this wild goose chase, all because of some woman he had no right to care about. Spencer nodded as he made his decision; they needed to go back to looking after themselves. They couldn't keep putting themselves in danger for other people, no matter what they were being paid. Then again, there was the fee. If they played this week right, then they could be set up for a long time, not have to worry about money ever again… Or at least, not for a few weeks…

The carriage jerked to a halt, pulling Spencer out of his thoughts as he was forced to jump down to the ground to allow the door to open. He stared at the closed door as Mr Davis stared back at him from within until he realised that he was expected to open it. Biting back the urge to complain about being treated like a manservant, Spencer opened the door with a flourish, bowing his head enough to make the point but not enough to be pulled up for being insolent.

Mr Davis stepped down, glaring at Spencer, followed by the other man. He was very tall with long black hair and a neatly trimmed beard. His gaze passed over Spencer and he shivered as it did so; the man's eyes were two pits of perfect blackness. Spencer stared at him, open-mouthed, his heart pounding with a terror which he could not fathom. Then the man blinked, and Spencer saw that he was instead staring back at him with perfectly normal brown eyes. The man passed by, leaving Spencer questioning his own vision and sanity. Maybe it was just the way the light had hit the man's eyes, he said to himself. Yes, that must be it. Even so, there was something familiar about the man. Where had he seen him before?

"Wait here," said Mr Davis before turning to hurry after the other man up the steps of a nearby house.

"What's goin' on?" asked Bart, appearing next to Spencer.

Spencer shrugged. "We're to wait 'ere."

Ten minutes later, the door opened and the man emerged,

144

followed by a young woman who was staring fixedly ahead, her movements determined but jerky, as though she were being controlled by strings pulled by an invisible puppeteer from above. Mr Davis was close behind, and from inside the house came the sound of shouting.

"You can't do this! I won't let you go!" A man burst out of the house, trying to get at the woman but his progress deliberately delayed by Mr Davis.

"Keep him back," Mr Davis said to Spencer and Bart. "Meet us back at the Society." They stepped forwards to stand in front of the protesting man. He tried to push past them, but a firm hand from Bart held him off and he watched helplessly as the carriage, with the woman inside, clattered off down the street.

The man's shoulders slumped, and he sank to the ground. Spencer and Bart looked at each other and then down at him.

"Sorry, mate," said Spencer. "But we had to do as that man said."

"Don't worry though," Bart burst out before Spencer could stop him. "We're not really workin' for them. We're tryin' to find out what's going on so we can help people like you."

The man looked up at them with the kind of desperation which would allow him to believe anything, no matter how ridiculous, if it helped him. He looked from one to the other of the two roughly dressed thugs. "Really?"

"Yeah, kind of," Spencer said slowly, glaring at his friend. "We need to know: what just happened here?"

"That was my wife," the man said. "Over the past year or so, she started seeing and hearing strange things. The dead, she said. She could hear them speaking, see them appearing in rooms at all hours. At first, I thought it was just flights of fancy, but she carried on and so I asked the family doctor to see her. He said that she had contracted some form of mania and gave us some medicine which made it worse. I was at my wits' end until I saw the advertisement for The Thaumaturgical & Paranormal Society. I thought they would be able to help me." He let out a short laugh. "Instead they ignored me and as good as kidnapped my wife."

"But she walked out of here of her own accord," Spencer said.

The man shook his head. "As soon as that Mr Emerson took her hands and looked into her eyes, it were as though she were hypnotised. She stopped listening to anything I said and… Well, you saw how she was when she left the house."

Bart frowned. "I've got a question. I get what 'paranormal' means, but what about 'thauma-tur-gical'?"

"It's from the Greek," said the man. "It means magic, or rather, using magic to change things in the physical world." He frowned. "Hang on, who did you say you two were?"

Spencer grabbed Bart's arm. "Thanks for your help, sir, but we need to be off now. We'll do what we can to get your wife back as soon as." They quickly marched off down the street before the man could ask any more questions.

Chapter Twenty

"There you are," barked Mr Davis as they approached the building. "You took your time, didn't you?"

"Needed to make sure that man didn't follow you," said Spencer. "'Ere, that girl—she all right?"

"Never you mind about that girl; she's none of your business. See these crates? They need loading into this carriage." He stomped away.

As they moved over to the crates piled up at the side of the road, Spencer hissed, "I told you: we should've made our escape while we could. We should warn the girl, tell her to get the hell away from anything her husband's planning, take our money and run."

Bart shook his head as he picked up one end of a crate. "You go if you want. I'm stayin' until we find out exactly what they're doin' here, so we can stop it."

Spencer stared at him. "You're not some knight in shining armour, you know! You're the same as me: a no-good scruff from St Giles'. Our place is grafting at the bottom, keepin' ourselves out of notice so we can earn enough to get by, and hopefully at some point escape the streets. We're not the types who should be putting ourselves in danger like this for other people."

"A girl's in danger. We can't just run away and leave her." Bart stared pointedly back at him.

With a deep breath, Spencer picked up the other end of the crate and helped manoeuvre it into the carriage. "Not right," he muttered to himself. "We should cut our losses and run; this is far too dangerous."

"Don't worry," said Bart as they continued their work. "We'll be fine. No one knows us, we're just a pair of labourers, right? We do a bit more work, see what we can find out, then disappear. All safe, like. And we get paid for it, too."

"I suppose you're right," muttered Spencer. He glanced at the nearest crate and noticed the address stamped onto the top. "Huh. Victoria Dock. Small world"

"That's where we were the other day, right? Wonder if that golem unloaded this crate."

Spencer replied with a brief "mm", his brain whirling with possibilities.

They turned to gather another crate, only to come came face-to-face with Lord Marchant, with the dark-haired Mr Emerson at his side.

Spencer and Bart both dropped their heads, hoping that the man would not recognise them.

"You two!" said Marchant. "I remember you from the coffee house; you were the idiots with that demon hunting poster. And you were outside my house earlier. What…?" He turned to Mr Emerson. "These men work for you? Why are you having me followed? What is this outrage?"

Mr Emerson cast a cold eye over the two men. "I assure you, my lord, that I knew nothing of this. But we will get to the bottom of this."

Spencer shot a sideways glance at Bart. "It's all goin' to be fine, yeah?"

*

Spencer and Bart were pinned against a wall in a small box room by four thugs. Mr Emerson stood before them, glaring, as the door was flung open, Mr Davis flying through breathlessly.

"What's going on?" asked Mr Davis, his face flushed with panic.

"I understand that you hired these two individuals?" asked Mr Emerson, his eyes fixed on the two prisoners.

"Yeah. Just this morning. Why? What have they done? I told them not to go poking their noses anywhere—"

"How did you come by them?"

Mr Davis looked from Spencer and Bart to Mr Emerson, blinking rapidly. "They turned up at the door. Old Jack let them in and told me we had two new recruits. I didn't know anything about them, never seen them before…" His sudden pause and deepening red in his cheeks betrayed him.

Mr Emerson turned and advanced on him. "You had never seen these two before, and yet you gave them a job, just like that?"

Mr Davis took a step backwards. "No, that's not quite right. I knew of them: I knew their old boss, a decent bloke from back over Seven Dials way. He was a stand-up bloke, so I just assumed…"

"Oh, you *assumed* did you," sneered Mr Emerson. "And did this old friend of yours vouch for them at all?"

"Ah. N-no," stammered Mr Davis. "You see, he got sent down."

"So what reason did you have for thinking that they would be worthy additions to our workforce, eh?" Mr Emerson took another step towards the man. "If they are from Seven Dials then I assume that they are crooks. Their former boss has been imprisoned—"

"Hanged, actually," said Mr Davis, immediately wincing at his own stupidity in interrupting.

"Did you have any way of knowing that they were not spies? Or someone sent here to meddle in our affairs, sent by our… competitors?"

Mr Davis's mouth worked silently, opening and closing for a moment before he managed to say, "I don't understand. What's happened?"

"What's happened is that, immediately before they came here to seek employment, they were seen loitering around outside the house of our esteemed client here, and before that following him around." Mr Emerson gestured to Lord Marchant who was glowering silently in the corner.

"But—" started Mr Davis.

"Silence," snapped Mr Emerson. "Go and wait in the yard. I shall decide what to do with you later."

Mr Davis meekly walked out of the room, shutting the door gently behind him.

Spencer found himself wilting under Mr Emerson's cold gaze. "Now that you've had time to think about it," the man said to him, "how about you tell me exactly who it is that you are working for, and what you are doing here?"

"Let me guess," said Spencer, sounding much more confident than he felt, "if I tell you what you want to know, you'll let us go and we can forget all about this. Except you won't, will you?"

Emerson shrugged. "I'll hurt you a lot more if you don't tell me. You have no idea how much pain we can inflict on you."

Spencer licked his lips, his mouth suddenly very dry. He looked over at Bart, who was pleading him with his eyes not to say anything; not to betray the girl.

Spencer remembered another of his father's words of advice: *"If you're ever trapped or in trouble, find the quickest way to save your own skin."* His every instinct was screaming at him to do this, to just tell Emerson everything and hope that that bought them enough goodwill so that they could find a way to escape.

But then he caught Bart's eye again, and saw the mixture of hope and warning there. His friend was not above doing something stupid under normal circumstances, but given the attachment he'd developed to the girl… Spencer shuddered; he was going to have to do something unthinkable. Something very stupid.

"Don't know what you're talking about," Spencer said, hardly believing the words were coming out of his own mouth as he lifted his head up slowly to stare back at Mr Emerson. "We was just looking for work, right Bart?"

"Right," rumbled Bart from beside him.

"Don't you have any ways to force the truth out of them?" asked Lord Marchant. "What about that process you showed me earlier?"

Mr Emerson tapped a finger to his lips. "Maybe. Although that does have a tendency to create rather permanent changes, which are unpredictable in their timing. If we lost them before they were able to tell us the truth, then…" His mouth stretched into a thin grin. "I wonder how stubbornly virtuous you would be feeling if you knew what we could do to you, what horrors we could visit on you in this place. We wouldn't just torture and kill you. Oh no, nothing quite so quick and easy as that. We have creatures here which can change you in ways you never dreamed possible: not in your worst nightmares."

Thankfully he was interrupted by Lord Marchant, who surprised them all by exclaiming, "My wife!"

Mr Emerson kept his eyes fixed on the two prisoners. "What do you mean?"

"Tessie—my wife—she has been acting very strangely these past few days. I told you that she was starting to suspect something, about her hysterical displays after the séances we used to test… Anyway, she has been more and more suspicious of my comings and goings; until today, that is. And then I suddenly find these two loitering outside my house and then again here!"

"So you think that your wife has employed them to keep tabs on you and find out what you're planning?"

"It… seems logical, does it not?" Lord Marchant's voice wavered as he stared at Mr Emerson's back. "She was with me when I encountered these two for the first time in the coffee shop. She would have seen the poster they had, advertising their services, such as they are."

Mr Emerson stared at Spencer and Bart for a moment and then his grin broadened. "I have yet to meet a man who could hide his emotions from me. A rather useful skill I picked up on my travels in India. Some people fight very hard to conceal their thoughts, but you two are like a pair of open books. I do believe, my dear Lord, that you are correct. Your wife has become so desperate that she has hired these two imbeciles." He spun round on his heel and marched toward the door. "Your lordship, we need to accelerate the process. We shall go and get your wife now before she does anything even more stupid."

Marchant gaped at him. "Now? You mean…?"

"Yes. I know that we wanted to wait a while longer, to prepare her and allow time for her to come round to our way of thinking, but the vessel is as ready now as it will ever be. More power may be needed, but that is a trifle which I can overcome. The carriage is loaded, the equipment is primed. We leave immediately." He opened the door and then stopped, glancing at Spencer and Bart almost as though they were an afterthought. "We have no more use for them," he said to the guards. "Take them to the Madam and make sure that someone is there to record the results. This should be a very interesting experiment."

The door banged shut behind him.

Chapter Twenty-One

Spencer and Bart were pushed and dragged along the landing to a door at the far side, one they had not noticed before.

"What's going on?" asked Spencer.

"You're going to meet Madam," sneered one of the men. "I think she'll be mighty hungry. It's been a while since she last had any guests."

Bart struggled against his captors, managing to fling one off of him but being rewarded by three others piling on to subdue him. "You don't have to do this, lads." Bart's muffled voice came from under the pile of bodies.

One of the men holding Spencer shrugged in part apology. "I'm afraid we kind of do have to do this. It's dog-eat-dog, you see? If we don't do what that man says... Well, we'll find ourselves in your shoes in no time."

A man in a long dark suit pushed past them, pausing to peer at the two men. "Are these the subjects?" he asked. "Good, they will suffice perfectly well. Give me a moment to make ready."

He opened another door to reveal what had once been a sitting room but now had as its centrepiece a small round cylinder which appeared to have been fixed to the floor by some form of rubberised material, out of which protruded a curved tube. The man pulled a chair up to the cylinder and sat down, peering into one end of the tube. After rotating it a few times, he grunted and placed a paper and pencil on a table to the side of the cylinder. Checking his pocket watch, he started scribbling, muttering to himself as he did so. "Time: 5pm. Subjects: two lower working-class men of indeterminate age…"

A guard unlocked the door in front of Spencer and Bart and swung it open to reveal the dank smell of a basement. Spencer and then Bart were forced down the cold stone steps into the murky gloom below.

Spencer glanced around as they reached the bottom of the stairs and, as his eyes adjusted to the darkness his heart sank as he recognised occult symbols on the walls, ceiling and floor. They were written in a dark substance which he was pretty sure was blood. At the bottom of the stairs was a chalk line, which extended all the way round the outside of the basement.

"'Ere," muttered Bart. "Don't this look a bit like that demon writing?"

"I'm afraid it does," said Spencer.

"What do you think that means, then?"

"Nothing good…"

In the centre of the room was a chair on which sat an elderly lady, dressed in clothes which had clearly seen better days. The remnants of a shawl lay on her shoulders, the once fine material reduced to a stringy rag which lay loosely over a 'Sunday best' dress which had been torn, battered and smeared into a tattered, muddy mess. At least, it looked like mud in the basement's faint light.

She turned her head to watch them approach, her eyes glistening hungrily.

The guards kept a wary eye on the old lady as they manoeuvred their prisoners to the bottom of the stairs, taking care not to touch any of the inscriptions on the floor.

"Stand here," a guard barked, pushing Spencer and Bart back against a wall.

"And if we don't?" Spencer asked.

"Then we'll all die."

"I thought we were goin' to die anyway? Isn't that what you brought us down here for?"

The soldier nodded. "Yes. You are. But I don't want to die with you."

"I don't want to die either," Spencer pointed out.

"For God's sake," snapped another man, who was bending over the nearest part of the chalk line. "You'll stand there because we say so, and because if you don't then we'll give you a damned good beating. And that goes for asking any more stupid questions."

The other three guards pressed closer round the two prisoners, as though to emphasise the point. Spencer glanced at Bart, his mind whirring with possibilities. They could take advantage of the guards' caution around all those chalk marks to create a diversion, a bit of confusion which might give them a chance to escape. However, before he could put any of that into action, the guard by the chalk line straightened up.

"That's it: push 'em in," he said.

They found themselves being propelled into the centre of the circle, the guard muttering and drawing something in chalk on the floor behind them as they passed. They felt their hairs stand on end as they passed through that barrier: a combination of the spell invoked by the guard and the thick atmosphere which surrounded the old woman.

The air was charged and tense, as though there was a huge storm brewing. Every breath took a huge effort and the thickness around them seemed to seep into their bodies, making moving and thinking a struggle. The old woman drew herself to her feet, leering at them with a cold intent. Spencer and Bart turned back, and the guards raised their guns.

"You try and come back here, and we'll shoot you," said one of the guards.

Spencer bit back the rising panic and looked around, fighting to keep his mind working. His eyes landed on a pair of corpses lying to one side, dried-out husks which gaped at the ceiling in silent screams. What had that woman done to them? Was that going to be their fate as well?

He shook himself. This wasn't helping.

Everything about the old woman and the precautions the guards had taken screamed some sort of demonic possession, although this wasn't any sort of demon he'd come across before. He'd heard rumours about Wraiths which stalked the countryside and sucked people empty from the inside-out; maybe that was what was inside this woman?

He allowed himself a brief spark of congratulations at his powers of reasoning, although that did not really solve their problem. He looked around frantically, at the guards hiding behind their chalk line, the marks and symbols on the wall and floor, the glass tube through which the man upstairs was watching them. He was probably enjoying it, too. What he'd like to do to that toff ponce…

Think, Spencer, think!

"These people here," he said, indicating the corpses. "They went the same way we're going to, I take it?"

"That's right," said one of the guards.

"What if we fight back? You fellas goin' to come in and restrain us?"

The guard raised his eyebrows. "You mean step over that chalk line? No fear. We'll stay where we are, thank you."

"Why don't you make it out of paint?" asked Bart, joining Spencer in trying to shrink away from the old woman.

"What?" the guard seemed upset that they wanted to talk, rather than gibber and scream in terror.

"Chalk's easy to rub off. Paint lasts longer. If I was going to have some special writing to ward off demons, I'd use somethin' that wouldn't get rubbed away by someone's foot." He shrugged. "Just seems like a bit of a flaw in your design, that's all."

The guard pulled a pistol out of his waistband and cocked it. "Try anything funny, and I'll fill you with lead."

The idea hit Spencer like a thunderbolt. He looked at the chalk circle and then the other designs around the room, clearly intended to keep the demon contained in that room.

"Just need a distraction," he muttered. "Bart. Remember back in St Giles, when them two blokes did for that demon with a steel pole?"

Bart turned his head slowly to look at him, tearing his eyes away from the old woman who was advancing on them terrifyingly slowly. "Yeah?"

"Well, there's a poker over there. Reckon you can do some damage?"

Bart turned to look at the advancing creature. "But that's an old lady. Could be someone's Granma…"

"That someone's Granma's goin' to eat us alive if we don't do for her first! Look at her: there's nothin' human left in there!"

Bart blinked and then nodded, picking up the poker while Spencer darted over to the other side of the room, pulling a jacket off one of the corpses and trying not to notice that a stick-like arm came with it.

The old woman cast her eyes from one to the other of them, confused by her prey separating. Luckily, Bart's instincts kicked in.

"Oi, over 'ere!" yelled Bart, clanging the poker against the wall.

As the old woman turned at the noise, Spencer noticed with satisfaction that the guards started to panic, straining to see whether Bart's banging had dislodged any of the charms or markings. Maybe this plan would work after all.

"You see, lads," Spencer said to the guards, "I don't know much, but I do know that these chalk circles stop working if they're broken by anything passing over the top of them. Like a bullet, for instance. Which is why I know you're bluffing when you say you'll shoot us if we do anything funny."

The looks on their faces was all the answer he needed.

"I'm guessin' that those poor souls whose bodies are lying

down there knew that, if they broke the circle, they'd be dooming loads and loads of other people to a horrible death," continued Spencer. "That's the sort of thing good people do. Noble sacrifice and all that. Problem for you lads is I've never been a good person, and I don't intend to start now."

He sprinted to the tube sticking out of the ceiling and spat on it, rubbing away at the symbols which had been painted on and around it. Then he ran to the far side of the room and did likewise with the chalk line on the floor.

"What are you doing?" screamed one of the guards. "Stop that. Stop him at once!"

Spencer ignored him. "Now, Bart—now!"

Bart had been moving slowly away from the old lady, drawing her round the circle in a lumbering dance. At his friend's cue, he threw himself at her, plunging the poker straight into her chest.

Spencer ran back over to the observation tube and smashed the glass opening with his elbow. He shouted—"Gaaarrrgh!"— partly as a cry of triumph and terror but also to mask the pain now searing through his arm.

Bart, meanwhile, found himself nose-to-nose with the old woman. Blood bubbled from between her lips, and her eyes cleared as a yellowy-white mist seeped out from her skin. "Thank you," she croaked, a faint smile of relief touching her mouth before her body went limp. A mist seeped from her body, like the morning dew rising from a field on a cold day.

The mist swirled around and then, noticing a chance to escape, headed straight for the perimeter of the room, flying through the gaps Spencer had made in the chalk circle. The guards started backing away and up the stairs, eyes wide and teeth gritted in terror. The mist plucked at them and then looped back and flew straight across the room at Spencer and Bart.

Both men threw themselves to the floor, covering their heads with their hands and holding their breaths as they braced themselves for a pain worse than any they had ever experienced.

It never came.

They glanced up to see the mist disappear through the broken glass in the viewing tube, and a few seconds later heard the sound of running feet and screaming from overhead.

Spencer let out his breath and levered himself upright. "Well, that worked out all right," he said, his voice shaking.

Bart was already moving across the room towards the stairs, picking up a chair and growling at the few guards who had not yet fled as he advanced on them. The men stared at the murderous expression on his face for a moment and that, coupled with the sounds of terrified struggle from above, decided them. Glancing up at the door, they turned and sidled away and around the sides of the basement.

"Look, mate, we're not going to do anything, all right?" said one of the guards. "We're just going to sit here until whatever's up there is finished. So we won't get in your way if you want to leave."

Bart turned to Spencer and shrugged. "What you reckon?"

Spencer looked around, shivering. "I want to get as far away from this place as possible."

"Yeah. We've got to warn Tessie. I mean, Lady Marchant."

"Bugger the girl. I want out of here. Let's go."

They paused at the top of the stairs, listening to the sounds of struggle which seemed fainter and more subdued.

"We run," Spencer said. "As fast as we can, we just run. No matter what we see. Got it?"

Bart nodded grimly and then they burst out the door, making straight for the outside. But in spite of their best intentions, neither man could resist a glance in the rooms they passed.

The first room, where the smartly dressed man had set himself up with the viewing tube, looked as though a riot had swept through it. All the furniture had been upended and smashed against the walls; even the door to the room had not survived the destruction, hanging in splintered tatters from the frame.

They heard moaning coming from a room further along and glanced in to see a scene from a charnel-house; blood and flesh splattered across the walls and floor while bloodied bodies lay prone, some still moaning lightly. Screams and the thump of people running and throwing furniture resonated from somewhere above.

Whatever had come out of the old lady had been angry. And hungry. Very, very hungry.

During their mad dash, it felt as though the hallway had lengthened by a few miles, as though they would never reach the front door. Eventually they came within touching distance of the outdoors, although Spencer feared that, at any moment, they would feel the cold touch of whatever it was that was causing so much chaos throughout the house.

As he ran, Spencer breathed a panicked chant: "Oh shit oh shit oh shit oh shit…"

They burst out into the street and dashed up the road. Spencer glanced back to check that nothing was following them, finding his eyes instead drawn to the sign by the door.

"Oh…" he said. "I've been an idiot…" His mind made up, he turned to run, only to find himself colliding full-on with the brick wall which was Bart, the impact sending him sprawling to the ground. He glared at Bart as he picked himself up. "What're you doing?"

Bart was staring at the house, its seeming stillness at odds with the chaos within. "We did that. It's our fault."

"No," Spencer shook his head. "They did it to themselves. They're the ones who turned that woman into… whatever it was they turned her into. And they're the ones who tried to lock us up in there with her. And it's worse than that. They've done lots worse."

"What do you mean?" asked Bart.

"It's been staring us in the face all the time. The name. Think about it: Thaumaturgical and Paranormal Research Society."

Bart shrugged, pulling a face.

"Take the first letters. T-A-P-R-S. Tappers."

"You mean…?" Realisation slowly dawned on the big man's

face.

"Yeah. It was all true after all. The Tappers do exist. It's that lot, and they've been snatching women and doing their weird demon ghost magic on them. They deserve everything they get."

"Even so," said Bart. "We were the ones who let her out. All that blood… it's down to us. And there could still be folk in there who didn't do wrong. Maybe some of the women who were snatched. We've got to help them; we're supposed to be goin' straight."

"You're forgetting something really important, mate: for the likes of us, it's dog-eat-dog, and always has been. That's the mistake they made: assuming we'd stick to their rules."

Bart frowned at him. "Shouldn't we do somethin'? Go back in there and…?"

"And what? Get ourselves killed as well?"

"It's not right," Bart muttered, starting back towards the house.

"Bart! What are you doing? Get back here right now! What about… What about Tessie? You heard them: they're going after her…"

His words had no effect; Bart turned and broke into a lumbering run back towards the house.

Spencer cursed to himself. "Of all the days he decides to grow a conscience, it would be this one, wouldn't it?" He shook his head, clenching and unclenching his fists. "This ain't right," he muttered. "There was a reason we ran out of that place. Them demons could rip us to pieces…" He let out a frustrated howl as he watched Bart pull open the door to the house and charge inside, before breaking into a run himself.

Chapter Twenty-Two

Spencer almost collided with Bart again as he pushed open the front door. His friend was stood there, an immovable rock, mouth open as he tried to make sense of what was around them.

When they had left, just minutes before, the building had been in the process of descending into chaos, but what they were now faced with was nothing short of hell on Earth.

Doors had been torn off their hinges and lay strewn around the hallway. Furniture and boxes had been reduced to not much more than splinters, and there was the thick smell of iron and sulphur in the air.

"Bugger," said Spencer, looking round wide-eyed. "We shouldn't be here."

"This was our fault," said Bart. "We need to fix it."

"Think back to what happened," said Spencer through gritted teeth. "Remember what we're dealing with? Demons. Great big murderous demons. You don't run into a fight with them sort, do you?"

"I thought we were the demon hunting agency. Isn't hunting demons exactly what we should be doing?"

"The one time in his life he decides to use logic," muttered Spencer. "It would be now, wouldn't it?" He put a hand on Bart's arm. "If there's profit in it, then we get involved. Here there ain't profit; only a very painful death. Now come on: let's get out of here. Again."

A scream from upstairs caused Bart's head to twitch round. "Not until we've got all them lot out. Come on!" He ran up the stairs before Spencer could protest further.

Spencer stood there for a moment, turning his head to look from the stairs to the door and back again. A bellow from Bart at the top of the stairs made up his mind. "I must be going mad," he said through gritted teeth as he forced himself into a run, up towards the sound of battle.

He reached the top of the stairs and immediately slipped in a puddle of slick blood, crashing into the wall in a groaning pile.

"Come on, mate, don't just lie there!" yelled Bart. He thrust a shaking, blood-stained girl at him. "Get her out of here, I'll find any others and get them to you. Savvy?"

"Savvy," said Spencer, any affront he may have felt at being the one taking orders for a change overwhelmed by relief at being given a purpose in that hellish chaos. The girl was frozen in panic, unseeing eyes staring wide. The same girl they had helped Marchant snatch from her husband, only hours earlier. Although now it felt like days, or even years, ago.

"Come on, love," said Spencer. "Let's go!" She turned her head to face him, but it was clear she had no understanding of anything around her. Whatever she had seen, it had robbed her of all her senses.

Spencer muttered a curse and manhandled her down the stairs and out the door, turning to see another person—a man this time—being pushed towards him. He held open the door and beckoned frantically. "Come on, this way. Let's go!"

He lost count of the number of people he encouraged, pulled and shoved out of that hellhole. But finally there was just one left, a panicked-looking old man in a smart suit being roughly pushed by Bart.

"I need to contain them!" The old man yelled in a high-pitched voice.

"Get him out of here," bellowed Bart as he propelled the man forward.

"No!" yelled the man. "If we leave it like this, they'll escape and then who knows what will happen!"

"Hold on, Bart," Spencer said. "He's got a point." He turned to the old man. "You know what to do to stop this?"

"I do," the man nodded frantically. "But we have to move fast; it may already be too late!"

"Fast is good," said Spencer. "What do you need to do?"

"I need to get back to my laboratory, where this great lump pulled me from. I have the necessary items there to contain this."

"Back... In there?" Spencer balked.

The man nodded and, before Spencer could protest, Bart had yanked the man round and was pushing him back towards the stairs.

"Wait!" The man shouted, pulling a piece of paper out of his pocket and thrusting it at Spencer. "Draw this symbol on the door: it is a seal that will buy us time, trap them in here. Then bring that paper back to me. I shall need it for the rest of the spell." He turned and started up the stairs.

"Wait!" said Spencer. "I don't have anything to draw with."

The old man and Bart both pointed to the floor. "Plenty of stuff there," Bart said.

"What...?" Spencer looked down. "You mean the blood? You can't be..."

"Do it!" the old man shouted over his shoulder as he disappeared round the corner of the stairs.

Spencer pulled a face as he stared down at the blood-soaked floorboards. "They must think I was born yesterday," he muttered, looking around for something—anything—else. A howl from the depths of the building decided it, and he plunged his finger into a nearby puddle and started scrawling.

After a minute, he stepped back to admire his handiwork and then frowned as he looked up the stairs. The sounds of otherworldly chaos cascaded down towards him, a threat of something terrible just out of sight. He looked down at the scrap of paper in his hand and then back upstairs, shaking his head slowly. He put his hand on the door handle, his breath coming in short, sharp bursts. Then he looked at the seal he had drawn and realised that, if he broke it, there'd be nothing stopping the ghouls in the house from following him out as well.

He cursed again. "Why didn't I draw it on the outside of the door? Idiot!" He looked round. "So I either run out there chased by a load of murderous thingies and doom my mate, or I stay in here, trapped with them," he muttered. "Great choice. Thanks for that, you two." With a deep breath, he threw himself up the stairs before he had a chance to change his mind.

Reaching the top of the stairs, he turned and then pulled to a swift halt as he felt something wet land on his head. He put his hand to his hair and then frowned as he bent down to inspect the dark, sticky mess on his fingers. The lack of light made it difficult to see, but as he held it to his nose there was the unmistakeable metallic scent of fresh blood. A part of him marvelled that, even though he was in the middle of what had now turned into a slaughterhouse, he could still smell fresh blood. He looked up.

Spencer had always thought of himself as pretty worldly-wise, someone who had seen the best and the worst that life had to offer. He had been in some of the toughest gangs in London's East End and, while he'd never personally done anything too rough, he'd been in the room plenty of times when bad stuff had happened. Really bad stuff. Not only that, but he'd been around more than his fair share of demons, watched the world nearly end—at least twice—and had been within spitting distance of more massacres than he cared to remember.

But this was different. This wasn't just casual slaughter; it wasn't just random and vicious carnage. It was something more: a massacre by a creature that not only enjoyed the killing, but wanted to make some sort of statement as it did so. The scene on the ceiling was a macabre work of art, something which he could not pull his eyes away from, no matter how desperately he tried to do so. As far as he could tell, the congealed mass of limbs and bodies up there had once been at least two people, maybe as many as three or four. A couple of faces screamed lifelessly down at him, framed by limbs and torsos arranged in a manner that would have been almost beautiful, if it wasn't so horrifying.

He was snapped out of his stupor by another bloody gobbet landing on his forehead. Resisting the twin urges to vomit and run screaming out of the building, he wiped his face, swallowed down the fear, and pressed on.

He ran down the corridor, looking left and right with feverish intensity until he found Bart standing guard over the old man, who was working frantically at a desk.

"Here," said Spencer, throwing the scrap of paper at the old man. "Now can we go?"

"Not yet," the man said. "I need to finish this. Help your colleague."

Spencer turned to Bart. "Help you with what?" he asked.

"Keeping all them away," said Bart, nodding at the hallway.

Spencer turned and peered into the gloom. "I don't see..." he started to say, but then the words caught in his throat as he started to make out shapes in the darkness. He squinted. There was no form to what he could see, just a mass of indistinct suggestions of things which hinted at horrors lurking just around the corner, out of sight, like the hidden creatures that haunted his childhood nightmares, the monster under the bed, the ghoul behind the bedroom door.

The not-seeing was the worst of it. A visible threat was one he could have dealt with: run away from or find a weakness in. But an unseen one could be anything: huge and monstrous or small and swift.

He swallowed hard, moving back so Bart was between him and whatever was out there. "I came through them, didn't I?" he said in a hoarse whisper.

"Yeah," said Bart. "I was pretty impressed you made it through. They didn't seem much interested in going for you."

"And you didn't think to warn me?"

"What good would that've done? You'd've only stopped running. Then they'd've definitely got you."

"But I came through..." Spencer flapped his hand at the malevolent shadows, suddenly feeling an uncontrollable urge to scrub his shuddering skin.

"You were perfectly safe," said the old man. "The runic symbols on that paper you were carrying will have protected you from them. As will the symbols I have traced around the entrance to this room. For now, at least. Now, you, Mr Spencer, is it? Please come here and lend me a hand."

"It's just 'Spencer'," he said, stepping over to help. "Bart's also capable of helping, you know."

"I am sure he is," smiled the old man. "But I am a firm believer in matching peoples' abilities to the tasks at hand. Mr Bart there is very much the sort of person you would always want to have between yourself and any form of danger. Whereas, from the look of you, I would deduce that you are the more cunning of the two of you."

Spencer shrugged. "I suppose you're right. What do you need me to do?"

"I am going to perform what we in the trade call an 'exorcism', following the instructions in this text." The old man held up a sheet of paper which was covered with scrawled text. "If we do it correctly, that should not only contain all these confounded creatures, but also send them back to where they came from, where they can no longer do us, or anyone else, harm."

Spencer squinted at a picture which had been underneath the sheet of paper. A print of a red book cover with an image of a devil on it. "That looks familiar. Is it the sort of thing you'd see all over the place?"

"Hah! Quite the contrary; it is an incredibly rare text. Only a handful are in existence, and as far as I am aware this is only one of two in the whole of England. Or rather, the original is, which is I believe in the hands of Mr Emerson."

"Yeah, I met him. He's your boss?"

"In a manner of speaking. Anyhow, we do not have time to discuss book collecting—I am not sure how long my protective runes will keep those creatures out. Come, help me arrange these candles. I am Mr Culpepper, by the way. Cornelius Culpepper."

As Spencer followed the instructions, Mr Culpepper peered at him. "I understand from Mr Bart that you two were responsible for the unleashing of these creatures upon us."

"Hang on," said Spencer. "That's not quite true. We were trapped in a basement with some creature, and it was a case of kill-or-be-killed. We did what we had to, to survive."

"Hmm. Quite a price was paid so you two could survive, don't you think?"

Spencer shuddered as he remembered the blood-soaked corridors. "We did what we had to do. And anyway, it wasn't us that put the ghosts or demons—or whatever they are—in this house in the first place. I'd say that, in the grand scheme of things, we're the last people who should have fingers pointed at them."

Culpepper inclined his head in agreement. "You have a point. And yet you both came back in here to help out."

Spencer nodded uncertainly. "Well, you know, we did what was right. We couldn't just let people…" His voice trailed off as he felt his cheeks redden.

"Many would not have done that, so I applaud you both. And you have given me the opportunity to put this all right, once and for all."

"So you were one of the ones who brought them here? These blood-thirsty ghosty things?"

"The correct terminology is 'wraiths'," said Culpepper. "And yes, in the interests of scientific investigation, myself and my colleagues brought and contained a number of them here for study."

"I'm no expert," said Spencer, "but seems to me your scientific studies aren't strictly what right-minded people would look on as strictly kosher, you know?"

Culpepper sighed. "I know. And it was not intended that way; we started this institution as a way of furthering mankind's understanding of the various malign forces that we now find ourselves sharing our world with. Understanding them so we may better know how to protect ourselves from them. We never meant any harm."

"So what went wrong?"

"As is so often the way, one bad apple spoilt the whole bunch."

"Emerson."

"Mr Emerson indeed. You said that you met him."

"Him and Lord Marchant. They were the ones who trapped us with that wraith, trapped in the body of some poor old bird."

Culpepper looked up, tears flecking the corners of his eyes for a brief moment. Then he handed Spencer another candle, indicating for him to place it in the far corner of the room. "Yes. That was an unfortunate implication of our work: the particular genus of wraith that we have been working with seems to find it difficult to manifest in our realm in any meaningful manner."

Spencer raised an eyebrow. "Them things out there don't seem to be having too much trouble manifesting."

Culpepper shot him a wry smile as he handed him another candle, gesturing for him to place it next to its fellow. "Indeed. But what they are doing right now is more chaotic and primal, less contained. Think of them a bit like the air. When it is left to its own devices, and in particular when it is whipped up into a frenzy, it can become highly damaging gales. But trapped in a jar it is perfectly harmless: controllable and capable of study."

"So you were using old ladies as jars to hold your wraiths? That sounds… really bad. And anyway, the one we was trapped with didn't seem too harmless to us. She tried to rip my face off!"

"Yes, well, my analogy wasn't completely perfect. We were in the process of trying to find a way to make the process work for both host and wraith."

"Host," sneered Spencer. "You make it sound like they had a

choice in all that."

"Well they did," protested Culpepper as he scrawled with chalk on the floor. "All were volunteers. They were approached because they had strong propensities towards the paranormal: they were extremely sensitive in relation to sensing and communing with ghosts and other spirits. They were excited—honoured, even— to be a part of this…"

"Did they know what it would mean?"

"In what way?"

"Did they know what they were letting themselves in for? Did they know they'd be letting something like them things out there into their heads? Did they know how much it'd hurt?"

Culpepper blinked at him. "Hurt? What do you mean?"

"The one we went face to face with, down in the basement. When I smashed the lettering to free the wraith, the old woman, before she died, thanked us for doing it. The whole thing killed her, and from what I saw it wasn't a pleasant experience for her."

Culpepper put a hand to his forehead, muttering quietly as he breathed deep, shaking breaths. After a few moments he cleared his throat and then nodded. "We are nearly finished. Pass me the sheet of paper, please. The one with the incantation on it."

Spencer frowned but still did as he was asked. "You know," he said, looking again at the print of the book's front cover on the table. "This book cover's really very familiar."

"Unless you are an expert in arcane literature, I very much doubt it."

"Arcane? I thought this was a magic book?"

"It is. Well, not really a 'magic' book, but that is probably the closest description for a layman. It is a book of spells and incantations, one of which I need for our current purposes. Now, please stand beside Mr Bart there; I require all this space for the spell."

Spencer did as he was instructed, joining Bart at the entrance to the room, both of them watching Culpepper as he thumbed to the correct page and started chanting in a hesitant voice.

"You know what this reminds me of?" asked Bart.

Spencer rolled his eyes. "Mate, you know this is really the wrong time to start a chit-chat?"

"Was just thinking," grumbled Bart. "All this stuff reminded me of that time we watched Thaddeus do that spell. Same sounding words and stuff."

Spencer turned to stare at his friend but, before he could say anything, Culpepper's voice moved up in volume and the air seemed to change around them.

"Stay perfectly still," Culpepper boomed, his voice sounding as though it was coming from right next to them, not from the other side of the room in the middle of a so much more powerful than just a few moments before. "I have erected a protective field around you, which will ensure that the wraiths cannot harm you. You just need to stay inside the circle. Do not step outside until all of this is over. To do so would be fatal!"

They looked down to see that they were standing inside an elongated chalk circle.

"What about you?" Spencer called back to Culpepper, but his voice was lost in the growing chaos around them. They could only watch as Culpepper chanted, his words buffeting them as they tore into the creatures infesting the house. The air around him seemed to take on substance, the screams of the ethereal demons being sucked into the room forming a hellish cone around him, which as time went by became more and more solid. "How's he going to get out?" Spencer muttered.

Culpepper's chanting became less ordered and more ragged as he seemed to grasp at breaths, the effort clearly taking a toll on his body and mind. Through the swirling mists, they could see his face contorted in painful concentration. The vapours enveloping him obscured him once more, only to part once more to show him on his knees, his face a rictus of pain as he continued to force the words out of his mouth.

"We've got to help him," Spencer said, starting forward.

Bart stopped him with a firm arm around his body. "You

heard what he said: we can't step outside this circle."

"But look at him: he's dying!"

"And he still will, even if we go to him. Only difference is we'd be dead too! You're the one who's supposed to be good at thinking. So think: he put us in here to keep us safe. We're no good to him if we get ourselves killed as well."

"But why'd he do that?"

As though he'd heard their words, Culpepper looked straight at them with bloodshot eyes, tears streaming down a face which seemed to be being torn to pieces in front of them. Then he bellowed one last word.

The room exploded around them, a chasm opening for what was less than a second. But in that second it sucked out everything: demons, vapours, furniture. Everything except for the two men stood in the safety of their protective circle.

"Is it over?" asked Bart, his voice sounding unnaturally loud in the sudden silence.

They looked around: there was nothing except the sounds of the house settling once more.

"I think so," said Spencer, taking a hesitant step outside the circle. He winced as his foot passed over the chalk and landed on the other side. When nothing happened, he let out a breath and ran over to the old man's body.

He was little more than a wizened husk, all life sucked from his body.

"You stupid man," Spencer said. "Why'd you do that? Why save us?"

"Because we can still do some good," said Bart. "We need to sort this. Stop what him and his mates started." He turned and ran out the room.

"Wait," shouted Spencer after him. "Where are you going?"

"Tessie," came the reply.

Spencer groaned as he forced himself to follow.

Chapter Twenty-Three

Tessie sat in her sitting room, pretending to read a book in the candlelight. She did not know who she was trying to fool with her masquerade; she was alone in the room and had been since the maidservant had placed the pot of tea on the side table and retreated to the kitchen, half an hour beforehand.

She shifted in her seat, took another sip of tea, and then frowned down at the words on the page. Her mind wandered as soon as she did so: to the encounter with those two rough men, her heart rate increasing as she remembered how she had felt when running with them from the demons, how she had helped them all escape. In those moments she had felt something she had never experienced before: a feeling of excitement, of elation, of being alive. But it was more than that: for a brief period of time, she had been a part of a team. She had mattered. For once, her voice had had equal weight.

Until they had gone off without her. That still hurt: that she had been cast aside so easily by them. But they had had a point; they could not do the work she needed them to do, to spy on her husband, if they had her in tow. But she found herself constantly thinking back to those odd, dirty men, to the adventures they were having, the freedom they enjoyed. It took an effort of will to fight against the urges of every fibre of her being not to jump up and go out in search of them.

The front door banged, jolting her from her thoughts. It was him. She clenched her fists and forced herself to breathe as normally as she could, her chest suddenly tight. She focused once more on the pages in front of her, scrutinising each word in the hope that they would provide a gateway to a different, safer, happier world.

She managed to not flinch as the door to the drawing room slammed open. She kept her gaze down, hoping that if she ignored him, he would just go away.

"Good afternoon, Tessie," Marchant said, his voice seeming harsher and more jarring than usual.

She looked up, contorting her face into as pleasant a smile as she could muster. "Good afternoon, husband," she said.

He walked over to her seat and took the book from her hands, turning it over to examine the cover. "Have you had a pleasant day?" he asked.

"Yes," she replied nonchalantly. "Rather pleasant."

"You do not seem to have made much headway with your book."

She shrugged. "I have done other things as well. It was not so long ago that I sat down to read."

"Oh? What other things? Did you take a walk perhaps?"

He knew she had. The butler would have told him everything. "I did."

"Meet anyone interesting?"

"Not particularly."

"No. Of course not. That was yesterday, was it not?"

"I… I do not know what you are referring to."

"It was rather interesting," Marchant said, pacing to the window. "There are a couple of ruffians who I keep seeing. Do you recall the fellows I am referring to?"

"Not particularly," she said, keeping her voice level, almost bored. "You always tell me to not bother myself with such things."

"Indeed. But I keep seeing them. Or rather, *kept* seeing. They will not be bothering us again. Or anyone else, for that matter."

Before she could stop herself, Tessie let out a gasp.

Marchant spun round to look at her. "What an interesting reaction for people you claim not to recall."

"It's just... I... was shocked by your form of words. Do you mean to say there has been a terrible accident?"

"There has. Very terrible. But do not fret: all will now be resolved." He raised his voice. "Mr Emerson?"

He stepped through the door: the tall, thin man with a pinched face which made him look as though he were viewing the entire world with disdain. He looked round, then his gaze settled on Tessie and a thin smile split his face. She felt a shudder run down her spine and she found herself shrinking back in her seat, almost willing herself to disappear from view.

"Good day, Lady Marchant," the man said. "So good to see you again."

Chapter Twenty-Four

As he ran, fighting to keep pace with his friend, Spencer's mind kept flashing back to the terrors they had only just managed to escape from. Emerson's dark eyes seemed to leer at him from around every corner, while his imagination kept conjuring up the vision of the hungry old lady and the wraith-like creature which had possessed her. At any moment he thought that he could feel the cold tendrils wrapping around him, ready to drag him back to that horrible place.

At least they were running away from that damned building, and he planned to keep as much distance between himself and there from now on. No more of this stupid heroic rubbish. Spencer cared for only one thing; that him and Bart kept away from the demons—or whatever they were—and the people who had brought them into this world.

He cursed himself for coming up with the idea of a demon hunting agency in the first place. What was he thinking of? They were way out of their depth, and all he cared about now was putting as much daylight between him and his friend, and the mess they'd blundered into.

Bart skidded to a halt as they approached Jermyn Street, pulling Spencer to one side. He pointed at the Marchants' house, outside of which stood the carriage they had loaded up just a little while earlier.

They ducked into the shadows, watching as the door to the house opened and two men emerged—Lord Marchant and Mr Emerson—followed by two guards carrying the limp body of Lady Marchant.

"Tessie," murmured Bart, starting forward.

Spencer held his friend's arm in a grip tighter than he'd ever thought possible. To run over there, with all those men around them, would just guarantee a quick and painful death. He remembered Emerson's dark eyes, the way they had seemed to bore into his mind back in that house. Maybe he was a demon as well; that would certainly explain a lot.

The thought triggered something in Spencer's mind, bringing back memories of being trapped in that house. He felt the panic rising even further, Turning his whole body to ice-cold stone. His breath came in short, sharp bursts, making his heart sound like it would burst out of his chest and the world around him seem sharp and otherworldly, as though he was watching everything through a strange, distorted lens.

Bart struggled against him, but didn't use anything like his full strength: either recognising the sense of not intervening, or not wanting to hurt his friend. They watched as the carriage started to jolt down the street back east, towards the river.

Spencer's mind was still abuzz with the visions of the terror they had left behind, which he wanted to never come into contact with ever again.

It seemed like an eternity before Spencer realised that Bart was shouting at him.

"We've got to go after it! Let go of my arm and come on!"

Spencer stared down, surprised to see his fingers clasped in a white-knuckle grip around the larger man's arm. Blinking, he opened his hand and stared at it as the world spun around him.

"Come on," snapped Bart, already starting down the street.

Spencer stared at him, marvelling how he seemed so far away and yet so close. Then he realised what Bart was saying, where he planned to go, and that shocked him back into the real world.

"No," he muttered. Then, louder: "No. I can't."

"We can't leave her. We've got to go after her." Bart glanced over his shoulder at the carriage which was almost at the end of the road. "I'm not losing her."

"No," pleaded Spencer. "You can't make me. We need to get as far away as possible. This isn't… We're out of our depth." Saying the words seemed to flick a switch in his head, a massive release. "It's not our place to do this sort of thing. We need to get away before it's too late."

"It's already too late," said Bart. "We're committed. All this is our fault; we've got to make it right."

"No. We've got to survive, and that ain't gonna happen if we follow that carriage. Come with me; we'll head somewhere safe, start again." A final thought struck him: the unthinkable. "We'll drop back the money she gave us, then we don't owe them anything. Please." He dropped to his knees, panting in panicked breaths. "Please," he whispered, tears picking at his eyes.

Bart stared down at him, open scorn on his face. He shook his head, and then turned and ran after the carriage.

"Please," whispered Spencer, unable to do anything but watch his friend run away down the street and out of sight.

*

Bart jogged, taking care to keep a good distance between himself and the carriage. For once, he was glad of the poor state of the London roads and the huge amount of traffic, as it meant that he didn't have to tire himself to keep pace, and could easily hide in the crowds. He toyed with the idea of launching a raid there and then on the vehicle, but quickly changed his mind: he'd only get himself arrested or worse. Better to bide his time and wait for them to make a mistake, hopefully somewhere less busy where he could knock some heads together without worrying about getting his collar felt.

He remembered Spencer kneeling there in the dirt, begging him not to go. He'd always relied on his friend to tell him the best thing to do, to keep him out of trouble and keep them both safe. But there, in that street, he had finally seen his friend for what he was: a coward.

He knew Spencer would argue that they owed Tessie nothing, that they should look out for themselves and no one else. After all, if they didn't look out for themselves, then no one else would.

But he also knew that he couldn't just leave the girl to whatever it was those men had planned for her. Maybe Spencer was right, and he'd gone soft on her. Fact was, he couldn't stop thinking about her, couldn't put her face out of his mind.

A memory swam to the surface, of another girl like Tessie, being dragged away all helpless, never to be seen again.

Tessie wouldn't disappear like his Ma did, all them years ago.

*

Spencer found himself pacing the street, clasping and unclasping clammy hands as he stared wide-eyed around him. He felt as though everyone was looking at him, expecting him to do something that he would never be able to do. Just the thought of throwing himself back into the line of fire was enough to send his heart beating so fast that he thought he would throw up.

He couldn't do it. He'd always been there for Bart, the pair of them like twins joined at the hip. In all the years they'd been together, this was the first time they'd gone separate ways. There was an emptiness at his side, like an arm had been lopped off.

This was stupid; Bart had always been a lumbering, impulsive creature. Spencer was the brains, the one who set things right through words and thoughts rather than brute strength. He'd be back soon enough, when he ran out of ideas and realised that running headlong into God-knew-what was as stupid as it was dangerous.

Spencer's mind drifted back to when they were loading the

carriage, just before they were captured, to the address which had been marked all over the crates. Victoria Docks. It was a remote place, wouldn't have too many people round it at that time of day. It was also hard to defend, far too many ways in and out. If a person made a big commotion, they'd be able to scare out anyone hoping for some peace and quiet to do mischief…

Of course, he had a pretty good idea of what sort of mischief the two men, Emerson and Marchant, were planning. His nerves were set even more on edge at the thought of Tessie turning into something as ravenously evil as that old woman had been. But not so much that he would willingly run alone, unarmed and unprepared into harm's way.

The answer hit him between the eyes, almost dizzying in its obviousness. Before he could talk himself out of it, he turned and ran, in the opposite direction from where Bart had gone.

Chapter Twenty-Five

Bart hunched down outside the building, leaning forward to catch a glimpse of what was going on inside. Through gaps in the wooden slats he could make out Tessie's prone form lying on top of a row of crates, while a dozen men busied themselves building some sort of huge structure under the watchful eyes of Emerson, while Marchant paced up and down nearby.

Bart's eyes flitted over the scene, sizing up his options and the chances of him being able to grab the girl and get her away from her captors and to safety. He shook his head; he needed help if he wasn't going to be overwhelmed within a few minutes of showing his face. But he couldn't leave the girl there, at the mercy of whatever it was they were planning.

He looked around, taking stock of his surroundings. He hadn't had a chance to really do so until now; he'd been concentrating on making sure he didn't lose Tessie and her captors. He knew they were at the docks, but hadn't really paid too much attention to exactly where. Now he could see that they weren't that far from where they'd robbed that man, only a few days before. He shook his head, amazed at how much had changed in such a short space of time.

He swore under his breath, partly at Spencer for being such a coward but also at himself for just blundering in without a plan.

He turned and looked around, wondering if he should go and try to drum up reinforcements; surely he'd be able to get enough people from the Dials to help him. If he showed them his fists, he was bound to get enough volunteers; if the chance to do a good deed for a pretty lady wasn't enough of an incentive.

It was no use. It would take him far to long to leg it over to Seven Dials and back. By the time he did get back, it would probably be too late. Listening to the distant sounds of workers in the nearby docks, he wondered whether he could convince them to help him. He shuffled away and round a corner so he could see where the nearest dockworkers were.

He paused, open-mouthed, as he caught sight of the massive, lumbering thing a few hundred yards away.

*

"There you are," said Thaddeus. "Been busy, I see." He was leaning against a wall just around the corner from what was left of the Thaumaturgical & Paranormal Research Society building.

"Could've done with your help in there, you know," said Spencer. "That sort of thing would've been right up your street."

The magician shook his head. "I told you before: I do not get involved in such matters."

"Even when it involves that book you were so bothered about?"

"What?" Thaddeus took a step towards him.

"Yeah. You see, that book Seth stole, the one you got worked up about back in the pub? Well, I think it's in the middle of all this."

"How so?"

"The man who Seth sold the book to; he's the boss here." Spencer gestured to the wreck of a building. "He's gone and stolen away the woman who we was working for..."

"Presumably that's where your colleague has gone."

"Yeah. We need to help her..."

"So you can get paid."

"Mainly, yeah," said Spencer. "Although given what we saw them do in there—gettin' demons to possess women and stuff—we kind of need to help her before he does somethin' nasty to her." Seeing the look on Thaddeus's face, Spencer added, "Look, I know we're not the nicest people in the world. We're crooks and all sorts. But there's a line, right?"

"Maybe…" said Thaddeus. "You say that they were engaging in demonic possessions?"

"Yeah. But really nasty ones with… Wraiths. That was it. That was what Mr Culpepper called them."

"Culpepper? You met Cornelius Culpepper?"

"Yeah. He was in there."

"And where is he now?"

"Dead. He dealt with the demons, using some spells he took from that book. The book what Mr Emerson has. Doing it killed him, though."

Thaddeus scratched his chin, frowning. "I'm not surprised. There is very powerful magic contained in that text." He looked sharply at Spencer. "Is the book still in there?"

Spencer laughed. "Nope. Anything left in there is either caked in blood or torn to pieces. But I do know where it is. You want it?"

Thaddeus frowned. "I may. Why?"

"I'm betting it's really valuable to a fella like you. The stuff you could do with it."

"What are you proposing?"

Spencer shrugged. "I'm not really proposing anything. Just musing, you know?" He clicked his fingers, as though the thought had just occurred to him, out of thin air. "Unless…"

"What?"

"I know where it is. If you help me get that girl safe, stop Emerson and his lot from causing harm to her, you can have the book."

"I won't engage in any battles. Especially not with Emerson."

"What?" asked Spencer. "You're afraid of him as well?"

"I am afraid of no man," snapped Thaddeus. "But there are certain things I will not do."

"All right," said Spencer, looking round. He rolled his eyes as he saw the two policemen, watching him from the other side of the street, then a slow smile spread across his face. He turned back to Thaddeus. "I've got an idea."

Chapter Twenty-Six

Bart peered in through the gaps in the side of the building. The people in there seemed to all be focusing on something on the other side of the room; the thing they were building looked like it was taking shape but was clearly at some sort of important point, needing all of their attention.

The main toff, that creepy Emerson bloke, was standing over the workers, occasionally barking orders. Meanwhile, Marchant was hovering around Tessie, clearly having been told to stand guard over her. For her part, Tessie was tied to a chair with her back to Bart, and hadn't moved in all the time he'd been watching. Bart wondered if she'd been drugged or knocked out. His fists tightened at the thought of those bastards having harmed her in any way. He had to do something.

His mind made up, he rose into a low crouch—or at least as low a crouch as his bulk would allow—and started to shuffle round to the door at the side of the building. After a few steps, his feet knocked a loose clump of rubble and he paused, holding his breath in case it alerted someone inside, before starting again. Stealth had never been his strong point, and it took all his concentration to make as little noise as he could.

After what felt like an age, he reached the door and slowly levered it open, tongue sticking out the side of his mouth in concentration. He couldn't believe his luck; all of those inside had their backs to him, seemingly oblivious to his presence.

There were a series of crates between him and Tessie, and the others: perfect cover for him to make his way over without attracting too much attention. Taking a deep breath, he scuttled over to the nearest crate, collapsing behind it, making sure his head was lower than the top of the crate in case anyone were to look over. He waited for a moment, ears straining to pick up any signs that he had been spotted.

He relaxed slightly as he realised that the sounds of people hard at work continued unaffected. He peered round the edge of the crate. Only four more crates and he'd be pretty much level with Tessie. Then, if he was quick enough he could grab her, although she looked to be tied pretty securely to the chair, and undoing knots was something he'd always struggled with. Fingers too big and chunky, that was what Spencer always said. If his friend was with him, he'd have had a much better chance…

Bart shook his head. Fact was, Spencer wasn't there; and the coward could go hang, for all he cared. He was on his own. If he couldn't untie the knots quickly enough, then he'd cut the ropes. Or just pick her up and carry her out: chair and all.

He reached down to his waist and then bit back a curse. He didn't have a blade on him. It must have got lost in the struggle in that house, or something. While he still fancied his chances against all of them in that building with his bare fists, a weapon would make it a lot easier.

He looked around, searching for anything which he could use. His eyes fixed on something shiny, not too far away.

Then he heard the sound of a gun being cocked. "Stand up, nice and slow," a voice said. "If you even think about swinging at me, I'll blast your head off."

Bart glanced around, his body tense as he weighed up the chances of him being able to reach the man before he was able to fire his gun. If he made enough noise and was threatening enough, he might scare him into spoiling his aim.

186

The man seemed to sense his thoughts and raised an eyebrow as he steadied his weapon. A click from behind Bart, then another, told him that there was no longer just the one gun trained on him.

Tessie twisted to look round and, recognising him, she gave him a tight-lipped smile, a small nod in thanks for him trying to help; although her tear-filled eyes showed that she was resigned to whatever fate they had in store for her.

The sight was too much for Bart, and he growled and took a step forward.

"Afternoon all," came a voice from the doorway. "Room for a small one?"

They all turned to see Spencer being thrust into the room by one of the guards who had been left outside.

Emerson leered at them as they were tied to two chairs.

"Make sure you tie the big one extra firmly," Emerson said.

Bart turned his head to glare at the guard fastening his bonds. "Ouch," he rumbled.

"You two are becoming quite the annoyance," said Emerson. "I do not know how you managed to get away from Madam, but I can assure you that you will not be so lucky this time. In our haste to get started we forgot to pick up any bait; I was going to send the men out to round up some vagrants, but it looks like we will no longer have to."

"What do you mean: 'bait'?" asked Spencer. He looked around wildly and it was then that he saw Tessie being tied to a cross, which was in turn secured inside a glass dome. An outline of spiky lines had been drawn with a sticky dark liquid on the floor around the glass dome. He wondered if it was paint, tar or some other substance which was being used to make the markings. Then he saw, just to the side, a goat lying on its back, head lolling at an angle thanks to the deep cut gouged in it's throat. "Oh," he said. He glanced back at Emerson. "Do us a favour, mate. I left my best pocket watch in my other jacket. What's the time?"

Emerson frowned. "The only thing you need to worry about, when it comes to time, is how little you have left."

Bart had also noticed what they were doing to Tessie, and started struggling against his bindings. Two men cocked their rifles and pointed them at his chest, while a third stepped forward and hit him across the face with the butt of his weapon.

Bart spat blood and glared pure venom at the man before turning to look at Emerson. "What're you doing with her?" he asked.

"You'll see," Emerson replied. He glanced at the men guarding them. "Make sure they don't move. If either of them causes any trouble, you'll be first on the menu. Before them. Understand?"

The men nodded, studiously avoiding Emerson's gaze.

Spencer and Bart watched Emerson march back towards where Tessie was being held, barking instructions and sending people rushing around in his wake.

"What are you doing here?" asked Bart.

"Come to help an old mate. Couldn't leave you to handle this all by yourself, could I?"

"I dunno. I'm still thinking of you back there on your knees, begging me to not come here. Makes me a bit suspicious to see you turn up here."

"I'm hurt. We're mates; I figured you needed help."

Bart snorted. "Help? From the likes of you?"

"What's that supposed to mean?"

"You know."

"No, I don't."

"I mean you're a coward."

Spencer shrugged. "Rather be an alive coward than a dead idiot."

"So why you here then?"

"Told you. Couldn't leave you on your own. That's not what we're about. You'd not leave me, would you?"

Bart grunted. "But you wouldn't come here without a plan." When he was met with silence, he added, "You've got a plan, right?"

"Dunno. Was going to see what happens."

"You came here, into all this danger, without a plan?"

"Well *you* did," Spencer pointed out.

"Yeah, but that's me: I'm expected—"

"Will you two stop bickering?" snapped one of the guards.

"So you got a plan?" Bart asked Spencer again.

"Why should I always be the one with a plan?"

"You're *always* the one who has a plan."

Spencer spat on the ground. "You're the one who rushed down here without stopping to think about what would happen, chasing your dick rather than thinking about your mate. Surely you had some sort of a plan?"

Bart shrugged. "Kind of thought I'd be able to barge in, hit a few people, grab her and then run out again."

Spencer barked a short laugh. "And you wonder why it's my plans we usually rely on."

Bart scowled. "So what's your big plan, then?"

Spencer shrugged. "The best time to ask would've been before you legged it over here, don't you think?" He looked up at one of the guards. "'Ere, mate, can you tell me the time?"

"You're annoyed with me, ain't you?" said Bart.

"Just shut it." Spencer bobbed his head in an attempt to get the guard's attention. "Mate, over here. Any chance of telling me what time it is?"

"Why?" the guard asked. "There an appointment we're making you late for?" The other guard chuckled.

"Manner of speaking, yes you are. Might be worth letting us go, before you get into real trouble."

The two guards smirked at each other. "You'd do well to keep your cake-hole shut," the guard said. "Or I'll shut it for you."

"You're jealous, ain't you?" Bart said to Spencer. "All of a sudden I'm not plodding after you all the time."

"Jealous? Of what?"

"Tessie. You can't handle the fact I've found another friend."

Spencer laughed. "If you think you and her'll ever be friends, you're stupider than I thought. She's a toff; she'll dump you as soon as she can." He shook his head. "You've known her all of five minutes and suddenly you're best mates. What about all the times you and I have spent together, eh? That not count for anything?"

Bart huffed in reply, suddenly conscious of the bemused smiles on the guards' faces. "What you lookin' at?" he snapped at them.

"Don't let us interrupt your little lovers' tiff," said one of the guards.

Bart struggled against his bindings again, while Spencer shook his head. "That's your answer to everything, ain't it? Use your fists."

"Well it's better than—"

Their attention was snatched away by a change in the air, a cold wave which swept across everyone and everything, freezing their thoughts and replacing them with a vision of the grave.

They looked over to Tessie. "Oh bugger," said Bart.

While they had been bickering, Emerson's people had finished their preparations. Emerson stood in front of the glass dome, reading aloud from the large red book in his hands. Marchant, on the other hand, was watching the treatment being meted out to his wife with a nervous intensity, itching to be a part but also keen to keep a distance, almost as though he felt that, if he didn't stand by the others, he could deny all involvement in what was to come.

Emerson paused in his chanting and turned to Marchant. "Before I commence the final section, do you want to say a few final words of goodbye to your wife?"

Marchant blinked at him, then registered the smile on Emerson's face, mocking him for his timidity.

Tessie glared at him. "Why?" she pleaded. "Why are you doing this? You promised my parents you would look after me. I am your wife!"

Marchant darted forward. "You have been nothing but trouble to me, ever since we wed. A pathetic excuse for a woman. You could have at least tried to fit in to society. Instead, you are an embarrassment. No wonder your parents were so keen to be rid of you."

"You… bastard!" she yelled, straining at the ropes around her wrists. "How dare you! After my parents… After you benefited from our family fortune! Without our money and influence you would be nothing! You…"

"I used you. Yes, I did. And it was so fortunate your parents both expired when they did. Such a stroke of luck, eh?"

She glared at him. "It was you, wasn't it? I always suspected, but…"

Marchant shrugged, a mocking snarl on his lips. "It's not as though they were wonderful parents to you. You told me as much."

"That is enough," said Emerson, gesturing for Marchant to step back.

Tessie struggled against her bindings as Emerson started chanting again, each word seeming to drive a dagger into her body, making her arch her back, twisting and turning as she desperately sought to escape their harsh touch.

Each utterance flung waves of despair at everyone in the room, wrenching at the edges of their very souls. Everyone hunched under the pressure from the attacks, like weary travellers caught in the jaws of a blizzard. Everyone, that is, apart from Emerson, stood in the eye of a malicious storm which had the tortured writhing figure of Tessie as its focus.

A few final sibilant utterings sent one huge blast across the room, blowing out the candles and plunging them into darkness, as though the sun had also been extinguished.

"Now would be a really good time for someone to tell me what time it is," said Spencer in the sudden, still blackness.

"Will you shut the f—" began the guard nearest to them. His words were cut off as the light started to seep back, although the

191

sight which emerged from the darkness made them wish it had not.

Tessie's face was a twisted mass of hatred, a parody which bore only a passing resemblance to the young woman she had once been. The creature's eyes flickered around hungrily, settling on the two men bound and helpless in the centre of the room. She—it—lurched forward, the bindings creaking as they struggled to hold her within her flimsy cage.

Bart once more started to struggle against the ropes around his wrists, while Spencer just glared at the guards.

"Could someone please just tell me what time it is!" he bellowed.

"Don't you think there's more important things to worry about?" Bart asked.

Emerson watched the mounting panic with amusement, flicking open his pocket watch with the air of a child teasing a starving animal. "It matters not what time you meet your end, surely. Whether it's five o'clock, six or two."

"So is it five o'clock?" Spencer persisted.

Emerson frowned at the face of his watch. "Just past the hour. Why is that so important to you?"

Spencer sat back and grinned. "Just wanted to know how long I needed to distract you idiots before this happened." He flashed a triumphant smile around the room.

Emerson and his guards all looked round the room as… nothing happened, aside from the girl-cum-demon snarling and struggling in the corner.

"Before what happens?" Emerson asked with a raised eyebrow.

"Give us a minute," Spencer said, glancing round. "You sure about that time you gave us?"

"Of course I am."

"Your watch not slow or anything?"

"Of course not. This is the finest Swiss craftsmanship, and my manservant winds it daily."

"You're sure you set it to the right time?"

"What sort of idiot do you take me for?" Emerson recovered himself. "I do not know what form of mummery you are planning, but I can tell you that it will not work." He turned and gestured to two of the guards. "Release the girl; let us see what she can do."

The guards rolled their eyes nervously, stuck between which they feared more: the slathering possessed creature, or the dark-haired man with the stern manner. Slowly, they edged towards Tessie.

"What are you dithering for?" Emerson snapped.

"She just looks a bit… hungry, sir," said one of the men.

Emerson sighed. "Are you wearing the charms we gave you? Good. Then she won't harm you—you will be no interest to her as long as you are wearing them. Now get to it before I remove that protection from you."

The men glanced at each other and then stepped slightly more firmly toward Tessie. Ever so reluctantly, they put their rifles on the ground and reached out to start to untie her bindings.

At that moment a few things happened.

The creature that had once been Tessie spat a venomous, curse-like sound at Spencer and Bart.

The guards jumped back. Then, emboldened that she did not seem to be concerned about them, leaned back in to continue untying her.

A thumping sound shook the room, a noise from outside. Something big was approaching them, fast.

"What…?" shouted Emerson, backing away from this newcomer.

"Your watch's slow," said Spencer. He looked up as two demons burst into the room, sending the door—and the guards standing by it—flying aside.

Bart groaned as he recognised them. "They're the demons what were after us. I thought we'd given them the slip."

Spencer grinned at them. "Bet you never hear this, but am I glad to see you boys." He twisted his head to the side. "'Ere,

Bart."

"Yeah?" Bart said in a weak voice, glancing sideways at his friend, who he was now convinced needed some special attention in the head department.

"You know we was wondering which would win in a straight fight: a demon or a golem?"

"Yeah?"

"I think we're about to find out."

The wall exploded inwards to reveal a huge man-shaped figure made of clay. The golem pounded into the room, straight at the demons which were advancing on Spencer and Bart.

Both men were thrown back by the golem's passage, their chairs splintering to pieces as they were swatted aside. Spencer's world flashed a bright red which tasted of copper. Everything seemed to slide along around him, and then he opened his eyes to see that Bart had pulled him to safety.

"You all right?" his friend asked.

"Think so," Spencer grunted. He looked up to see the golem pounding away at the demon. "So what d'you think of my plan?"

"What, nearly getting us killed by two demons and a big walking pot? Very nice."

Spencer spat out a sharp chuckle which stabbed at his chest. "Well, no point sitting round here. We need the book off that Emerson bloke. Reckon you can do that? Then, when you're done, see them guards trying to untie the girl? Why don't you stop them, and maybe relieve them of those charms that Emerson toff was talking about?"

Bart started toward the man then stopped. "What's the charms look like?"

"Dunno," shrugged Spencer. "To be safe, why not just take everything off them? Don't worry if you bruise them a little."

"Be my pleasure," grinned Bart.

Spencer started towards Marchant, who had been watching this fresh danger with increasing panic. Noticing Spencer's advance, he pulled out his pistol and shakily pointed it at him.

"Keep back!" he called out. "I'll shoot!"

Spencer slowed but did not stop. "You know, I've seen all sorts in my time on the streets. Gotten pretty good at reading people, seeing who's capable of what. The sort of person who can shoot a man… Well, that's a special sort of person. You need to be desperate, or have that certain something in you." He stared into Marchant's eyes. "You've got neither. You've had a nice comfortable life, and while you might be happy to order someone to do bad stuff, you've never dirtied your own precious, soft hands in your life. You won't shoot me." To prove the point, he put the palm of his hand over the barrel of the pistol, then gripped it and wrenched it from Marchant's grip.

He used the butt of the weapon to hit Marchant hard over the head and then grabbed at the chain around the man's neck and pulled it free, glancing at the charm it held.

"I'll have that." Spencer said. "You know how pathetic you are? You're the first person I've beaten by force for a long time." He rummaged through Marchant's jacket and pulled out a purse, heavy with coins. "I'll be taking that, too." He turned back to see Bart chasing the guards away from Tessie, who was thankfully still securely chained up.

The golem was wrestling with the demon, which in turn was desperately attempting to make its way over to Spencer and Bart. Thankfully, the golem was as strong as it was determined. Their battle took no account of such niceties as buildings or furniture, demolishing everything they came near and sending the guards scattering in their wake. Thankfully the fight stayed away from where the creature that wore Tessie's face was still straining against its bonds, still secured. For now.

Spencer backed away to the far wall, pressing himself back to avoid the flying debris.

"Why's it doing that?" Bart asked, nodding at the golem as he joined Spencer to watch the fight.

"Remember the piece of paper I said was rammed in its head? Ordering it to protect the humans? Back when we was nearly killed by the demons the first time, when we was down the docks, the golem got very interested as soon as they turned up."

"So you thought you'd gamble it'd do the same again," Bart said. "But how'd you know the demons'd turn up?"

"I kind've got the word to them that we'd be here at five o'clock."

"How'd you know demons can tell the time?"

"I…" Spencer blinked at him. "I s'pose that's a fair question. They still got here though, more or less on time."

"Yeah." Bart watched the fight in front of them. One of the demons was lying on the floor, prone, dark blue blood pouring from its head. The other one was still fighting, and was having a good go at tearing the golem limb from limb: literally. But the golem seemed to either not notice or not care about the damage, relentlessly pounding at its opponent. "Looks like we're gettin' our answer," he said.

"What's that?" asked Spencer.

"The answer to who would win in a straight fight. Golem every time. If it'd been the other way round, we'd be goners. Lucky, eh?"

"I planned all this; luck had nothing to do with it!" Spencer huffed when Bart grunted in reply. "Anyway," Spencer continued. "What happened to that Emerson toff?"

"He turned tail and ran," said Bart, looking around. "Me nicking his bracelet thing and giving him a bit of a kicking helped, of course. Looks like the rest of them decided to do the same, hey."

"Yep," Spencer said. "You get the book?"

"Yeah," said Bart, holding it up. "What you want to do with this?"

"I've got a buyer," said Spencer.

The demon had managed to back the golem into a corner and was in the process of pummelling him with clawed fists, dirty shards of pottery flying in all directions in the face of the onslaught. The golem lowered its head and charged forward, using the wall as leverage, and both creatures flew through the air. They landed in an awkward pile, the golem immediately pulling itself to its feet. The demon tried to do likewise, but then fell back, staring down at its chest in disbelief. There was a large hole, the size of the golem's fist, right where the creature's heart used to be. The golem stared back at it, impassive as ever, blood dripping from its hand. The demon collapsed and the golem turned to regard Tessie.

The sounds of the supernatural battle having stopped abruptly, Spencer and Bart turned their attention to also look at the possessed creature which wore Tessie's face, thankfully still held in place by what was left of her bindings.

"What do we do about her?" Bart asked. "We can't leave her like that."

Spencer patted him on the back. "Here comes the next bit of my plan." He walked over to the hole in the wall and whistled. A moment later, Thaddeus appeared.

"Where are the cops?" asked Spencer.

"Outside, arresting people running out of here," said Thaddeus. "They took one look in here and decided they would be better off staying out there. Can't say I blame them."

"Good," said Spencer. "Hopefully they'll be too busy to bother with us, then." He tapped his head and grinned at Bart. "Plan. See?"

"The book?" asked Thaddeus.

Spencer gestured to Bart, who handed it over.

Thaddeus nodded, thumbing through it, a distant greedy look on his face.

Spencer cleared his throat. "Our deal?"

"What?" Thaddeus looked up. "Oh yes." He peered at Tessie. "That's the one requiring an exorcism, I take it?"

"Yep. Anything we can do to help?"

"Don't get in the way." Thaddeus flicked through the book until he found the correct page.

"What's happenin'?" asked Bart.

Spencer glared at him. "I hope you're happy with yourself. You've made me break my one big rule: made me run towards trouble rather than away from it. And now I've gone completely against everythin' I stand for, and done somethin' heroic to boot."

"What do you mean?"

Spencer gestured at Thaddeus and then Tessie. "We're goin' to exorcise the Hell out of that bloody thing."

Chapter Twenty-Seven

"You sure about this?" Bart asked Spencer as Thaddeus started chanting. "Ain't this dangerous or somethin'?"

"I'm more than happy for us to stop and walk away, leave her like that all nicely caged up and demonic, if that's what you'd prefer."

"That's not what I meant. I just… Shouldn't we do somethin' to protect ourselves?"

"Listen," said Spencer. "If I start thinkin' about how dangerous this is, then I'm goin' to be following everyone else out that door. I've brought us a proper magician, as well as engineered a pretty genius escape plan, while you just got yourself captured. So don't start lecturing me…"

Bart held up his hands. "All right. Sorry."

The creature had been watching them hungrily as they made their preparations but, as Thaddeus continued to chant, it began thrashing around at its bonds, fighting to get free.

"Just keep an eye on it and make sure it doesn't do anythin' funny," Spencer muttered.

"All right," Bart grunted. He opened his mouth to ask a question, then thought better of it and stepped back to allow Thaddeus the space to do what he needed to do.

A tearing, cracking sound filled the room. They looked up to see the creature that once was Tessie finally pulling free from its bindings and breaking out from its prison in a mess of ropes and glass. It started towards them, a hungry look on its face.

"Oh balls," said Spencer.

"Leave it to me," said Bart, starting towards the creature. "You make sure he keeps doing his words and stuff."

"But it'll tear you to—"

Before Bart could respond, the golem stepped in between them and the demon.

"Oh no," said Bart. "That's worse. If the golem tears her to pieces…"

They watched, open-mouthed, as the golem bore down on the much smaller creature. It swung a massive clay fist down, which barely missed the Tessie-creature as it skipped aside. Another blow was dodged—just—sending shards of wood and stone flying around the room.

Suddenly there was an almighty screech as the Tessie-creature ripped a column from the side of the building and swung it at the golem's leg. The huge creature looked down, confused, as it suddenly found itself teetering on a shattered limb. The Tessie-creature then let out another howl as it launched itself at the golem's neck, ripping head from body in one swift motion.

It then turned to face Spencer and Bart again.

"All right," said Bart, stepping forward, holding his hands out at his sides. "I know there's some part of you that's still Tessie, yeah?"

"Bart, what are you doing?" hissed Spencer.

"Buying us some time," said Bart, running to the side, yelling at the creature to follow him.

The creature followed Bart, snarling, spittle flying from her lips as she stalked slowly toward him. As she passed the golem's prone form, she lashed out with a foot, sending yet more of the clay body flying in shattered pieces.

"Hey!" said Bart. "There's no need for that."

She hissed at him but still kept back. Then their attention was snatched away by a bellowed cry. They turned to see Marchant standing there, a pistol in his shaking hands. The gun was pointed, not at Tessie or Bart, but at Thaddeus.

"I know what you're trying to do," shouted Marchant. "But

it's too late. You can't undo this." He squeezed the trigger.

Bart yelled as Spencer launched himself in the air, between Marchant and Thaddeus, landing in a heap on the floor. Spencer looked down, his hand reaching under his shirt and coming out covered in blood.

"No!" yelled Bart. But before he could go after Marchant, he was overtaken by another form.

The Tessie-creature covered the ground to Marchant in a couple of paces, throwing herself forward in a savage blur.

"Wait," shouted Marchant.

The creature stopped, confused.

"You must remember me," he continued. "I am your husband. We made a holy vow to each other, to protect and serve: remember that? I made you what you are now: me. You owe me…"

While he was talking, Bart ran over to Spencer. "You all right, mate?"

"That bloody hurts," moaned Spencer. "I knew there was a reason why I avoided getting shot all these years."

"Let me have a look." Bart pulled aside his friend's shirt to reveal a mess of blood just below his shoulder. "Looks like he just winged you. You'll live."

"Easy for you to say," winced Spencer. "You being not shot and everything."

"Could be worse," Bart said, nodding over at Marchant and his attempts to reason with the Tessie-creature. She was staring at him with a look of vacant hunger on her face, cocking her head as he continued with his pleading. Then, with a roar, she threw herself on him.

"Ouch," said Spencer as he watched. "That looks really nasty."

"Yeah. I know he did some bad stuff to her. But shouldn't we, you know, try and help him?"

"Don't get carried away, mate. Just because we're doing good things for a change, don't make us *all* good. Let's face it: he deserves this."

Bart screwed up his eyes, his face paling as Marchant's screams became more liquid and less distinct. "She really was hungry, wasn't she?"

Meanwhile, Thaddeus's voice had risen in volume, echoing round the room:

"Regna terrae, cantata Deo, psallite Cernunnos,

"Regna terrae, cantata Dea psallite Aradia."

The Tessie-demon turned and snarled at him, moving away from what was left of Marchant's body. Bart picked up a knife and held it ready, not sure whether the weapon would do much damage if the creature did break loose, but just holding something lethal made him feel better.

"...caeli Deus, Deus terrae,

"Humiliter majestati gloriae tuae supplicamus..."

"It's workin'," Bart muttered to himself in wonderment, watching as each word seemed to stab into the creature's soul—assuming it had a soul to speak of, that is.

"Exorcizamus you omnis immundus spiritus,

"Omnis satanica potestas, omnis incursio,

"Infernalis adversarii, omnis legio."

A wind picked up around them, a cold chill which pulled at their clothes and hair.

"Omnis and congregatio secta diabolica.

"Ab insidiis diaboli, libera nos, dominates."

"Ut coven tuam secura tibi libertate servire facias,

"Te rogamus, audi nos!

"Ut inimicos sanctae circulae humiliare digneris,

"Te rogamus, audi nos!

"Terribilis Deus Sanctuario suo,

"Cernunnos ipse truderit virtutem plebi Suae,

"Aradia ipse fortitudinem plebi Suae.

"Benedictus Deus, Gloria Patri,

"Benedictus Dea, Matri gloria!"

The Tessie-creature had grown more and more agitated as he had continued and, with the last of these words, she let out an almighty shriek which made both men shrink away, screwing their eyes shut.

They glanced back up to see a malevolent screaming white mist flying out of Tessie's body. It circled the warehouse, darting from one corner to the next. It paused briefly at Marchant's corpse, before angling straight for the open door and flying out into the open air.

Spencer and Bart stared at the door, exhaling heavily together. The thought crossed both their minds that they should maybe go after the demon-spirit, but then their attentions were snatched away by a groan from Tessie's body.

"What happened?" she asked. "Where am I? Why...?"

"Bad men stuck a demon inside you," said Bart, helping her to her feet.

She put a hand to her neck. "I remember that man and my husband... Making me drink something... And then..."

"Yeah, well, they brought you here, to the docks," said Spencer. "Possessed you with a demon somehow, using all this stuff." He leaned heavily against the table, pressing his wound tight with his good arm.

"You're injured," she said.

"It's what comes from doin' a good deed," muttered Spencer. "First and last time."

She blinked at him.

"You saved me?"

"Yeah. Well, we all did. Including..." He turned to indicate Thaddeus, but the magician was no longer there.

Tessie looked down at the silent figure of the golem. "Is that...?"

"It's a golem," said Bart. "He helped us as well. Then you ripped his head off."

"Nothing a good kiln couldn't fix," said Spencer. "While I'd really appreciate you two finding me a surgeon of some sort, on account of me being shot and all?"

Tessie gingerly took a step forward, but her legs gave way

beneath her. Bart caught her.

"I owe you so many thanks," she said. "How can I ever repay what you have done?"

Spencer cleared his throat. "You've got a bit of stuff on your face. A bit of… your husband."

She put a hand to her cheek and pulled away a bright red globule of flesh, paling as she examined it.

Bart glanced over at the corner. "Oh, yeah, and you might have killed your husband." He gestured at the body.

She followed his gaze, staring blankly at what was left of the man's corpse. "Good."

Chapter Twenty-Eight

Seth stood, open mouthed, listening to the sounds coming from the warehouse building. He could see flashes of stuff through the holes in the walls that had been made by the golem and demons as they had crashed in, but it was the noise which froze him to the spot. Strange, otherworldly noises which made his blood curdle and his body itch to be anywhere but there.

It was a relief when finally it was over, replaced by a stillness which was almost as unnerving as the sound it had replaced. Then he saw someone emerge from the building and he found the strength to start moving again.

"You," he said loudly, running after the man. "What're you doing?"

Thaddeus paused and turned, fixing him with a cold stare.

"Hang on," said Seth. "I recognise that book. That's the one I sold... What you doing with that?"

"This," said Thaddeus, making Seth shrink away as he stepped towards him, "is not yours to sell. It is certainly not something to be placed in the wrong hands, as you did."

"Who are you to tell me who to deal with?"

"When it comes to items as powerful as this," said Thaddeus, "I am *exactly* the person to tell you. You have no idea what harm you did, selling it to Emerson of all people."

"He was the highest bidder," shrugged Seth. "Milton was

pleased."

"Milton is a fool, and so are you."

"Hang on," said Seth. "Remember who you work for…"

"I don't work for him. Not any longer. My debt has been paid in full."

"I reckon Milton will have something to say about that…." Seth blinked, confused. People didn't just stand up to him and Milton. That just wasn't done.

"Let him," snapped Thaddeus. "I no longer care. I have a message for him, and you, and any other goons you might choose to send after me. You do not know the full extent of the power I possess. And trust me: you do not want to find out." He turned and walked away.

Seth clenched his fists, reaching into his jacket and pulling out a knife. "I wouldn't walk away from me if I was you."

Thaddeus paused with a sigh and held up his right hand. He muttered something, and Seth suddenly found that he could no longer move. Then he watched with horror as the hand holding the knife started to move.

"After all you've seen me do," said Thaddeus. "After all you know I can do, and you come after me with a *knife*. Frankly, I'm insulted." He moved his hand and slapped it against his leg.

Mirroring Thaddeus's movements, Seth's hand whipped through the air, stabbing the knife into his own leg. He screamed in pain, dropping to the ground, thankfully now back in control of his body.

Thaddeus watched him as he writhed in pain. "Be thankful that I am rather drained from my exertions today, so do not feel the urge to properly make an example of you. Run along to your little boss and tell him I no longer answer to him. And if anyone comes after me, they will dream of me being as merciful with them as I have just been with you." He turned and walked away.

Seth gritted his teeth against the pain and, taking a few short breaths, pulled the knife out of his leg. He let out a low, keening noise, pulling off his jacket and tying it around the wound as tightly as he could manage.

"You look like you could use some help." A tall, dark man stood over him.

Seth squinted. "Mr Emerson," he said. "You… I tried to get your book back, but…"

Emerson shushed him. "I know. I saw. A rather bothersome man, that magician. But one sometimes has to cut one's losses. Live to fight another day, no?" He held out a hand, helping Seth to his feet. "Come," he said. "Let us get you some help for that leg."

"That's mighty kind of you, Mr Emerson, but I need to be getting to my boss."

"Ah yes, the legendary Milton. I will take you to him."

"That's all right," said Seth. "I can…" He tried to walk but his leg gave way as he started to try and put some weight onto it. He grunted and stumbled.

"Shush," said Emerson. "I will help you to get back. And then you will ensure that I have an audience with your employer. I believe Milton and I have common cause in many areas."

Seth blinked, a vague smile stretching across his lips. "Yeah. Of course you do. It's all right, isn't it?"

"Good fellow," said Emerson. "Now let us get going, before those two idiots in there come out."

"You're not afraid of Spencer and Bart, are you?"

"Afraid? No. But the next time I do see them, I will make them pay."

Chapter Twenty-Nine

"I know it's not much," said Tessie. "But I think this will do very nicely to start with, do you not think?"

Spencer looked around the set of rooms, larger than the whole space he and his folks had once shared with five other families. "And this is just for us?"

"Yes."

"What about this room?"

"Yes."

"And this one?"

"Even that one," giggled Tessie. "It's all just for you. Offices, meeting space, living quarters, and so on."

"It's too much," protested Bart. "We can't take this."

"Don't listen to him," said Spencer quickly. Then, louder, "We absolutely can take this!"

"But you've done enough already," Bart continued, ignoring his friend's glare. "You got that doctor to fix Spencer's wound…"

"But it is the least I could do, after my family trust wouldn't let me pay you what we had agreed. Money which you earned a hundred-fold at least. And if I can't pay you in money, then I will do so with the property I have in hand."

It had been Marchant's last laugh: in the absence of any other surviving relatives, his will had left everything to his wife, but on the condition that all expenditure be approved through a trust. A trust which did not consider paying Spencer and Bart's bill to be suitable expenditure. Particularly as none of them could produce a contract or bill for her to pay against—paperwork and formalities were not really specialities of either Spencer or Bart.

"Hang on," said Spencer. "Offices? Meeting space? What do we need stuff like that for?"

"Why, to continue your great work, of course," said Tessie. "That ghastly man—Mr Emerson—is still at large, is he not?"

Spencer frowned at her. It was true that the man—and the demon spirits he had conjured—had disappeared after the confrontation at the docks, and when they ventured back to The Thaumaturgical Society's building they found what was left of it had been hastily stripped and emptied.

"He has disappeared," said Spencer slowly. "Which can only be a good thing, right? As long as he's not bothering us?" He glared at Tessie and Bart. "Why do I get the feelin' you two are ganging up on me?"

"Because we are," said Tessie. "I will not allow anyone else to suffer the way I did, and the way you said those poor women in that house did. The authorities clearly do not see this as anything to bother themselves with, so it is left to us to ensure that whatever Mr Emerson is planning is frustrated, and the man is brought to justice."

"Hang on, hang on," Spencer held up a hand. "We're not that sort of people. We're just common crooks. We don't do any of that stuff."

"I beg to differ," beamed Tessie, placing a glass of champagne into his hand. "A respectable office, a wealthy benefactor, experience in successfully dealing with those fiends: I would say you are just the sort of people to do that sort of stuff."

Spencer looked helplessly at Bart, who shrugged in reply. "You said you wanted to go straight, get some good money, do somethin' different," Bart said.

Spencer glanced around the room, so much bigger and

warmer and cleaner than anything he had grown up with. A man could get used to this, he mused. And if he had to play at being detective for this madwoman to keep the roof over their heads, well…

"All right," he muttered. "But I'm not happy about this."

"Excellent," said Tessie. "A toast: to The Great Big Demon Hunting Agency." She chinked glasses with each of them. "Although we shall have to think of a better name."

Did You Enjoy This Book?

If so, you can make a HUGE difference.

For any author, the single most important way we have of getting our books noticed is a really simple one—and one which you can help with.

Yes, you.

Us indie authors and publishers don't have the financial muscle of the big guys to take out full-page ads in the newspaper or put posters on the subway.

But we do have something much more powerful and effective than that, and it's something that those big publishers would kill to get their hands on.

A committed and loyal bunch of readers.

Honest reviews of our books help bring them to the attention of other readers.

If you've enjoyed this book I would be really grateful if you could spend just a couple of minutes leaving a review (it can be as short as you like) on this book's page on your favourite store and website.

Acknowledgements

It's been a long time since my first novels came out, and almost as long since I had the germ of the idea that would develop into the book you now hold in your hands.

That it became a reality is thanks to so many people.

To Jess, Tom and Sam for your love, support and encouragement - I love you all more than you will ever know.

To Mum and Dad for your constant support, always.

And to my good friend, business partner, dev editor extraordinaire and all-round good egg, Simon Finnie. Cheers, Clem!

Thanks also to all the people who took the time to read advance copies and gave invaluable feedback which helped polish the story.

It's been a joy to write this first instalment in Spencer and Bart's story. Rest assured that Spencer, Bart and Tessie will ride again - very soon. But until then, if you want to see where it all began, cast your eyes over the next few pages to learn more about the murky world of the Infernal Aether...

Peter Oxley
Hertfordshire, February 2023

The Infernal Aether

The Aether always held the universe together… but in the nineteenth century, it just might tear it apart.

London, 1865.

Betrayed by his closest friend and rapidly drinking through his inheritance, sometime adventurer Augustus Merriwether Potts returns home to a world being torn apart by supernatural terrors.

A chance meeting with a mysterious stranger thrusts Augustus and his brother into a terrifying underworld of demons, ghosts, golems and clockwork men. An underworld controlled by a demon known as Andras, the God of Lies.

Andras has a plan: to bring Hell on Earth using the power of the Aether, a terrifying otherworld populated by creatures from beyond humanity's worst nightmares. With the world's governments in thrall to the demons, Augustus and his friends find themselves in the front line of a battle to save humanity against all the odds.

Dickens' London has never seemed so scary. *The Infernal Aether* is the first book in a gothic fantasy series which has been described as "no-holds-barred". If you like page turners with unpredictable twists and chills then you'll love Peter Oxley's *The Infernal Aether*.

The Demon Inside

How can you save the world when it's impossible to tell friend from foe?

Augustus Potts is in trouble.

The Fulcrum is fast approaching, an event that will tip the world into a new magical Dark Age and expose mankind to the full terrors of the Aether. More and more powerful demons are materialising on Earth, while neighbours and families are turning against each other thanks to the evil influence of the Witchfinder Generals.

While fighting the hell-hordes from the Aether, Augustus realises the runic sword that gives him all his supernatural powers is also turning him into the one thing he fears and despises the most: a demon.

At the same time N'yotsu, his friend and the one-time saviour of mankind, is realising that the only way he can survive is to turn back into the hated demon Andras.

When his closest friends and allies start to disappear, Augustus finds himself in a race against time to not only save the world but also himself…

In this most desperate of times, when the line between good and evil is not just blurred but torn to pieces, could his greatest enemy also be mankind's last hope?

Beyond The Aether

When Satan himself comes calling, what would you do?

In the summer of 1869 evil once again threatens England from the endless darkness of the Aether, with humans and their new supernatural allies locked in a battle for survival against the malevolent Almadite forces.

When the famed demon hunter Kate Thatcher is kidnapped by the enemy, Augustus Potts and his friends must risk everything—including the safety of the entire planet—to rescue her before she is lost forever.

Their quest will take them to the very edge of existence, to distant worlds beyond their worst nightmares where they must overcome an unholy entity that could destroy everything they hold dear.

Their only chance of rescuing Kate and saving mankind lies in forming an alliance with the demon Andras. But Andras has his own plans that could lead to him holding ultimate power over all creation...

If you could cheat the laws of time and space to save the one you cared the most about, would you do so—no matter what the price?

About The Author

Peter Oxley is an author, editor and coach who lives in the English Home Counties. He enjoys reading and writing in a wide range of areas but his main passions are sci-fi, fantasy, historical fiction and steampunk.

His influences include HG Wells, Charles Dickens, Neil Gaiman, KW Jeter, Scott Lynch, Clive Barker, Pat Mills and Joss Whedon.

He is the author of The Infernal Aether, A Christmas Aether and The Demon Inside.

He is also the author of the nonfiction book: The Wedding Speech Manual: The Complete Guide to Preparing, Writing and Performing Your Wedding Speech.

He lives with his wife, two young sons and a slowly growing guitar collection. Aside from writing and willingly speaking in front of large crowds of strangers, Pete spends his spare time playing music badly, supporting football teams that play badly, and writing about himself in the third person.

peteroxleyauthor.com
Twitter: @PeteOxleyAuthor
Facebook: PeteOxleyAuthor
Tiktok: @peteroxleyauthor

About Burning Chair

Burning Chair is an independent publishing company based in the UK, but covering readers and authors around the globe. We are passionate about both writing and reading books and, at our core, we just want to get great books out to the world.

Our aim is to offer something exciting; something innovative; something that puts the author and their book first. From first class editing to cutting edge marketing and promotion, we provide the care and attention that makes sure every book fulfils its potential.

We are:

- Different
- Passionate
- Nimble and cutting edge
- Invested in our authors' success

If you are interested in hearing more about our books, being the first to hear about our new releases or great offers, or becoming a beta reader for us, please visit:

www.burningchairpublishing.com

More From Burning Chair Publishing

Your next favourite new read is waiting for you…!

The Infernal Aether series, by Peter Oxley
  The Infernal Aether
  A Christmas Aether
  The Demon Inside
  Beyond the Aether
  The Old Lady of the Skies: 1: Plague

The Casebook of Johnson & Boswell, by Andrew Neil Macleod
  The Fall of the House of Thomas Weir
  The Stone of Destiny

By Richard Ayre:
  Shadow of the Knife
  Point of Contact
  A Life Eternal

The Curse of Becton Manor, by Patricia Ayling

Near Death, by Richard Wall

The Haven Chronicles, by Fi Phillips
    Haven Wakes
    Magic Bound

Love Is Dead(ly), by Gene Kendall

Beyond, by Georgia Springate

10:59, by N R Baker

The Other Side of Trust, by Neil Robinson

The Sarah Black Series, by Lucy Hooft
    The King's Pawn
    The Head of the Snake

The Brodick Cold War Series, by John Fullerton
    Spy Game
    Spy Dragon
    Burning Bridges, by Matthew Ross

By P N Johnson:
    Killer in the Crowd
    Run to the Blue

Push Back, by James Marx

The Blue Bird Series, by Trish Finnegan
    Blue Bird
    Blue Sky
    Baby Blues

The Tom Novak series, by Neil Lancaster
    Going Dark

Peter Oxley

Going Rogue
Going Back

The Wedding Speech Manual, by Peter Oxley

www.burningchairpublishing.com

The Great Big Demon Hunting Agency

Printed in Great Britain
by Amazon